RADIANT APPLES

JOE R. LANSDALE

Subterranean Press 2021

First Edition

ISBN
978-1-64524-041-9

Subterranean Press
PO Box 190106
Burton, MI 48519

subterraneanpress.com

Manufactured in the United States of America

For Tim Bryant

MY NAME IS Nat Love. I'm writing some things down. I'd like to start with a bit of philosophy that has sustained me on my life's journey.

You can fill a pot with piss quicker than you can with wishes, and with that thought in mind, you can most likely figure I'm not a wishful man.

Still, I got my hopes, if not my wishes. Lincoln may have freed the slaves, which my folks were, but Jim Crow still whips the colored folk's ass daily.

Things for me, in some ways, are better than many others of my color, certainly for the age I am now, and having said that, I want to charge in here and say right off with a lack of modesty, but with a large sweet custard of absolute truth, that I am a spry fiftyish man with all my parts working and my brain rolling on all its wheels, though from time to time they squeak and a dab of grease might be needed. I should also point out that I have some now and again aches from past adventures, and I pee a little more often than I once did, with frequent stops and starts, like a busy passenger train. I have also been known to slap a little bacon fat on an occasional rise of the piles, but the less said about that the better. Spry as I may be, I should admit too, that all the good that I am is less than the good I once was.

I have always had a better life than many of my color, because I took off and went West when I was just past being a boy. You could prove yourself out there, and though the color of your skin wasn't completely forgotten, less importance was put on it when a horse needed breaking, or they needed a Buffalo Soldier to ride out and shoot at Indians.

Even when I came back to the South, I had less restrictions than some, because along with Bass Reeves, another black Marshal, I rode the Arkansas hills, and on out into the Indian nation, and sometimes beyond. That gave me a bit of a rise in stature, at least for a time, due to I was known for chasing desperadoes that needed apprehended, often for hanging. Some had to be shot because they were wild and wooly about being arrested and I didn't want them to shoot me. Them that I laid low or led to a hanging I don't consider on much these days. They got what they had coming. I did my duty. End of story.

I miss the old days some, and a lot of the folks that lived it. Like shootists like Wild Bill Hickok, who I seen shot in the head in Number Man's saloon in the Dakotas. He was quite the character. And I miss the excitement of crossing the ocean with Buffalo Bill to perform in his Wild West show, once before the Queen of England. Think about that. Son of a slave sailing on the great waters to a land far beyond. The food there wasn't too good. Lots of boiled stuff, though their fish and taters were tolerable. Even there I could teach them a thing or two about how to make good double batter for fish, or most anything you might want battered.

I been meaning to write that story down, my time in Buffalo Bill's Wild West show, because it's full of adventure. I met people like Sitting Bull, Annie Oakley, and a peculiar fellow that gave me quite a problem, had a favoritism for knives and a hatred of whores. But that's another story.

Bottom line, there was a whole mess of others that was fascinating. So far, I haven't scribbled all that down in my crabby penmanship, and I suppose if I'm going to, I need to get cracking in due time. I can hear the old clock on the wall beating out the last of my minutes, because every day a fella wakes up, he's one day closer to when he ain't going to wake up.

That being a reality, I am making time to write down something that happened more recently, because I figure my kids, strung out as they are across the nation, might want to know of the old days, and how their old man lived then, but also how he has lived not so long ago as they went on about their lives. For me, it was somewhat like a trip back in time, this thing that happened, but with more soreness.

Only one of mine and Ruth's six children, young Rufus, went awry. The others have all gone up north and done well for themselves, and one of them is even a teacher. I know her mother would be proud, but she never got to see the end game on all of it. She's passed, and all I have of her are memories, nearly all of them good, and some of the best ones I have of her are from when times were the worst. She was my rock. Now and again, since she's passed, I think I can feel the ground shift under my feet. Maybe if she was here, she could do something about Rufus. He's the age I was when I run off from East Texas and went adventuring. I find it strange that I've come back here, living out on the edge of Big Sandy, Texas is no treat, but being on the job much of the time, it's not so bad. On the train I travel far and wide.

I remember when our Rufus wanted to be like me. Wanted to be a porter on a train. As he grew older that ambition shifted, which is fine, a fella must make his own path, but he was always driven to take the hard and long way around, venture down a trail you would think he could look at it and see was grown up with brush and weeds and full of snakes.

The empty trail, all clear and smooth, might lie before him with a sign that said SUCCESS, while the dangerous trail might have one that said, THIS WAY LIES MONSTERS, and sure enough, he'd veer off on the bad one. Learning from experience seemed a hard thing for him to grasp. He kept making the same mistakes over and over hoping for a different outcome that never showed up.

But still, I have hope for him. I will come to that.

There's been a lot of change since back in the old times, and some of it is good, though for me, riding the range and hunting down law breakers had a certain satisfaction that I can't find anymore. I liked living by my wits, when life and death sometimes depended on the quick pull of a six-gun, or a quick exit on a fast horse. Performing in Buffalo Bill's Wild West show came close to that feeling. Still, it was play acting, but since it was, you didn't actually get shot at. So that was a plus.

I'm not squawking about things as they are. Being a porter is hard work, but it's good too. Still, watching the country as seen through train windows, means it passes by too fast to enjoy it the way you might on horseback.

Nineteen-nineteen has its benefits. They come with the job I have, which though it isn't going to make me a rich man, pays better than picking cotton. I own me a Model T with an electric starter, got me a pop-up

toaster that toasts bread even and crisp, and in quicker time than it takes me to slice it. Something sad about those being thrilling things for me now, after all I saw and did when I was young.

I miss my wife, Ruthie, but I deal with feeling empty better than I once did. I still think about how lovely she was the first time I saw her, and how feisty, and how she talked to ducks and chickens. She said she spoke to them and they spoke back. I only heard chirps and squawks and quacks. Ruthie said she was able to translate, though some of the things she told me them birds said sounded suspicious to me.

At this point in my life, I look forward to retirement in some ways, and in other ways I hate the idea of it. I figure then it'll be me writing down all that's happened to me in my life, like I'm taking time to do now, and probably working a garden and walking in the woods, listening to the birds sing and the wind burp through the trees, shaking limbs and quivering leaves. Shooting a squirrel or fishing for bass for supper now and then. Perhaps, by the time I'm at that place in my life, that'll be good enough for me. But I sure hate to feel like I'm just waiting for the night.

Time I'm writing about now was a day that broke my heart. But I owe that bad day one good thing. It set me back on the path to adventure and a reconciliation of sorts. It started on a train.

I ride the Cotton Belt Line as a porter. The line is called that due to its hauling of cotton. Come through East and West Texas, and out the windows you see fields of white cotton growing in rows so long, if you were at the end of one, you'd need to send up a smoke signal to let those up front know you had caught on fire and was in need of a bucket of water.

Every box car stuffed with that fluffy white cotton holds the souls of colored folks in it, not to mention specks of their blood from the cuts them ole sharp cotton bolls can give a misplaced finger. When you wear cotton clothes and sleep on a bed stuffed with cotton, you are wearing or laying on the souls of those that plucked it for you. And sometimes those souls are screaming, even if you can't hear them.

—⁂—

NOW I'm coming to the murder and adventure part. It happened after the Spanish Flu came through the country like a big old tornado, killed a large patch of the population worldwide, and finally whistled out to nothing. Buffalo Bill was dead. The Old West was dead, and so were a lot of my friends.

But the Cotton Belt Line ran out of Big Sandy Switch, on into Tyler, and then Fort Worth, and I was on it. When you were nearing Fort Worth you knew you were about to be there by the sharp smell of cow shit on the wind, blowing in through open train windows, digging into your nostrils like a stinky mole.

I remember a white woman complaining of the stench, and her husband saying, "Honey, what you smell ain't cattle dung, it's money." Then he looked at me, said, "Ain't it, George?"

I nodded and smiled in a way that embarrassed me. I had learned to play the game, and I preferred to think of it that way, instead of kissing ass. My name is Nat, not George. The name was given to all us porters because George Pullman, who owned the Pullman cars he leased to the train lines, came up with the porter idea, a job exclusive to black men. He wasn't intending to be a savior to our race. He wanted cheap labor. And a colored man sort of disappears for a white train rider. They don't see us as important enough to matter. They talk about all manner of things around us, as if whatever is within earshot of us bounces off and goes away.

We slept when we could, four hours or so, in cramped conditions, and spent our waking hours making beds, trying not to notice men screwing women that weren't their wives behind drawn curtains in sleeping car bunks. We put drunks to bed, fetched hot milk for them that couldn't sleep, and everything else a body might want at any hour. This included making sure toilets were flushed out on the tracks while moving, instead of while stopped at a station, as that load could be messy and stinky to boot. I always locked the toilets up when we were in station to cut back on that nonsense until we were out and moving. I wouldn't suggest too many walks down or along the railroad tracks unless you wear high heel boots.

But I am straying in thought, as is acceptable for my age, I think. Let me just say I'm starting this story the night before it all began. I had swapped shifts with one of the porters I knew, so he could take time to get married. Night before I took his spot, I did something I rarely do before a day's work. I went dancing and skating and riding about. I also took my pleasure with a woman. A soiled dove named Lillian Francis.

I drove my Ford over to Tyler on that night, with the moon split in half in a starry sky. Over there they had a colored skating rink out in the back of nowhere, behind some buildings with poor lights. There was a shed party going on next to it, and I could hear music, and the lights were much better there, bright as the crack of creation. I parked across the street. There were only a few cars around, them being a bit expensive for most colored folks, and I felt some guilt about it, and at the same time I was proud of my being able to buy that car, show it off a bit.

I took off my bowler and put it on the seat, as I figured to dance some, and keeping that thing on my head would end up being my preoccupation for the night if I wore it, but I hated to abandon it, as I felt it gave me a touch of class.

I put the hat on my head, got out and walked over to the music, feeling good in my clothes. I was aging quite all right, I told myself.

The shed was also a kind of beer and barbecue joint, as well as a dance hall. It had once been part of a livery stable. It had open walls, a dirt floor, and a shaky tin and tar paper roof that hung over it all, supported on some termite-pocked post. Termites and sunlight are not known for their restraint. Folks had just come to trust that shed. If it fell, it would crush folks like grubs under a fat man's shoe.

During the day the tin and tar paper gathered up the heat and held it close, like a mother with a child. It was all right in the fall, which it was now, 'cause it felt good when the night turned cool, but in the summer all those warm, sweaty bodies and that tin and tar paper holding in the day, it could be hot enough that from time to time people would faint on the dance floor.

Next to the shed was the skating rink. It had open sides that could be closed by shuttering the walls and locking the shutters inside. The wood floor was polished and people were skating while listening to the music that sounded from the shed next door.

When I stepped on the dance floor, I realized the music was coming from Henry Thomas. He was sitting on a stool up front. A tall fellow with a forehead high enough a tick might need a ladder to get to his hair. He was there quite often, and was good to listen to, though there were days from all his traveling that it was best not to be down wind of him. He could get ripe.

When he was clean, the conductor sometimes gave him free rides on the train in turn for playing for customers, moving from one passenger car to another. Oh, how that music and his deep voice rang along those narrow corridors. I can hear it in my head even now.

Henry not only played guitar, sometimes sliding over the strings with a pocket knife, but he blowed into a set of hollow reeds he had on a rack strapped to his chest. They gave off a tweeting sound that damn near made you believe whistling haints was coming out of the shadows. Reels, jigs, old time yodels, country tunes and the like. He could do it all.

I hadn't no more than stepped under the roof, when Lillian came juking across the floor, doing a shimmy shake, and heavens she was cute in that blue, knee-high dress with the shimmy fringe on it. She looked like an ebony angel that worked cheap.

She knew she looked fine, and she shook it on up to me, and the next thing I knew, I was out on the floor dancing. By this time some trombone and trumpet players had showed up, and they joined in with Henry, and soon that place was hopping. Now and then I'd think about them termite-nibbled support post and that heavy roof, but for the most part the music took me away from worry, and touching Lillian's sleek body didn't do me no harm either.

We danced for quite a while, and then my age began to catch up with me. Not that I made note of it in front of Lillian, but I was glad I could talk her into going over to the skating rink. I paid for us some skates and away we went, listening and skating to the music, around and around, close together, holding hands, spinning each other about. I only hit the wall once and fell over twice. Lillian remained upright except for tripping over my fallen body once. She did a nice roll over me and landed on her ass. We both laughed.

The night rolled on, and finally we were in my car, motoring over to where Lillian lived in a walk-up shack. She wore my bowler as I drove.

—⧓—

UP in her room we never even turned the light on. She tossed my bowler onto a chair, and we started peeling one another, ended up in her brass bed with the squeaky springs, the firm mattress and the soft sheets. We made love. It was a paid for love, but it was good just the same, and wasn't that kind of quick thing I'd paid for back in the day with women who were looking at the clock, counting their money, and hoping I'd get it over with.

When we finished, we lay in the dark, propped up on pillows, and Lillian took to her nasty cigarette habit, lifted one from a little metal box on the bedside night stand. She lit it with a round lighter about the size of a baseball. There was moonlight drifting through the window and there was dust in the light, and then there was the curlicues of smoke from Lillian's cigarette.

"That was good," she said.

"Always is. Wait. You're not talking about the cigarette."

"Nope. Was I worth five dollars?"

"Worth ten. I'll pay you on my way out."

"No hurry. I like you here."

"I'm not rushing."

"We might go another round you want."

"I'll want."

"You was good, honey, but you seem a little off, like something's bothering you."

"I'm fine."

"Are you?"

"How do you know if I'm not?"

"You been fucking me long enough I can sense a mood. The job?"

"Job's all right."

"Am I going have to drop a rope down you and pull out the reason?" Then she hesitated, said, "I guess I shouldn't ask. I know I'm nothing to you."

"Don't say that."

"So, I am something?"

"Of course."

"A five-dollar whore?"

"You chose the work, Lillian, not me. I just give you work. But no. You're more than that. You're a friend."

"Just a friend?"

"Damn, girl. I never said I was looking to get married, and you got a healthy clientele, way you look."

"Well, you're getting old, Nat Love, and maybe you need someone to be around, to cook and wash and wipe your ass when you get even older."

"I'm all right. I cook good and wash good and wipe my own ass, and when I can't, well, I'll put a bullet in my head."

"If you can't wipe your own ass, you'll need me to shoot you."

"Listen, Lillian. I wanted to get married, I'd be glad to have you."

"Even though I'm a whore?"

"You can quit being one, learn a new trade. But I ain't looking to get married. I still love my wife, Ruthie. I miss her."

"One that talked to birds?"

"Chickens and ducks specifically. Thing is, I feel sort of like I'm cheating on her."

"Can't cheat on a dead woman... Sorry, Nat."

"It's okay."

"I mean, hell, it's a business transaction, that's all it is. Said so yourself."

"I'm an ass. You know it's more than that."

"I ain't going to tell you no sad whore story. Just saying I've made my way on my own a long time. My daddy, he got caught up in a cotton gin, ground into it. Wasn't a thing they could do for him, except put a bunch of bibles on him. That didn't help a bit, except for soaking up some of the blood. Daddy blew a big blood bubble, and when it popped, he popped off with it.

"They dragged him away and we put him in a wagon, me and my mother. I wasn't nothing but a kid. When we was taking him out of there, heard the boss man say, 'Hire another nigger. We still got plenty of day.' I knew then I wasn't working for the man all my days. I don't mean no offense by that, you doing just that."

"None taken."

"You're the famous Nat Love."

"Used to be the famous Nat Love, least in some tight circles. Now I'm just Nat Love, fellow who works as a porter. But I ain't complaining, Lillian. Far as jobs go, it's fine. I get more respect there than working a cotton gin, dragging a cotton sack. I do all manner of things on the train, including sometimes washing dishes when needed. But I'm somewhere between working another man's job and toting my own water. And I got that pension coming."

"Sounds cozy."

"I miss the old days sometime. That may be what you're feeling, me missing them."

"Your youngest boy ever write you?"

"No."

"I saw him in town the other day, Nat. Did he come to see you?"

"No. How was he?"

"He's all right, but he was with some colored and white boys that ain't worth the gun powder it would take to blow their asses up. I could just tell."

"He leans toward the malcontent and the trouble maker," I said.

Lillian sucked on her cigarette and let the smoke out in a circular cloud, said, "Lost his mama kind of young. Like me and my daddy. My mama, she went next, some kind of sickness. I think she just quit wanting to live, is what I think. I went wild myself. I mean, here I am in bed with a train porter giving it up for five dollars. Let me tell you something, Nat. Your son, he seen me. He knows what I do, and he wanted to buy some, but I told him I wasn't selling just then."

"Don't ever do that with him. Anytime he asks, I'll pay what he would have paid you, only don't do it. Tell me you won't."

"You think you have to ask? Come on, Nat. Listen, that boy is wanting to be special, like you. He wants to be the kind of man you were when young. I can tell that."

"I didn't spend my time with a bad crowd."

"Might be some would debate that, I bet."

She had me there. She rolled out of bed and put out her cigarette in an ash tray on the night stand.

"Lately, I've had this strong feeling for you," she said. "It won't go away. I don't want to do no other men. But it's either that or a cotton sack or putting berries in a can at the Lindale cannery. I wasn't made for either."

"You sure weren't."

"And this isn't all I'm made for either. I'm thinking on some new options."

"That's good. I said you could learn a new trade."

She was by the window, pulling the curtain wider. The moonlight bathed her sweaty, naked body and made her dark skin shine like damp obsidian.

"I've only stayed in this place last few years on account of you, Nat Love. Guess I been hoping for a little something outside of what we got, you know. But I can see that won't happen. I think I ought to catch a train. Ride with the chickens, fuck my way North."

"I wouldn't want you to go."

"I believe that. Just don't believe you don't want me to go enough. You'll miss me come nights like this, but there's other women, and most don't want anything but that five dollars. As for me, I'm thinking of raising my price, Nat."

I didn't respond to that. She came and crawled back into bed and pulled the covers up to her shoulders, rolled over and placed her arm across my chest. That second shot at the business didn't work out. She was quick asleep, and though I got there more slowly, I slept as well.

I T WAS STILL dark of morning when I dressed and put ten dollars' worth of silver dollars on her nightstand, next to her cigarettes.

I looked her over carefully, the bulk of her beneath the covers. I wanted to love her more than I did. I tip-toed out of there with my bowler in my hand, went home and put on my porter outfit, which was a white coat, black pants and bow tie, and the cap that identified our line with a shiny, silver plate on it. I also got my little two-shot derringer with a white ivory handle and tucked it in a little holster I had clipped to the back of my pants. It was such a small gun the coat covered it easily and without any real tell-tale sign of a bump. I hadn't never needed it, but I always sneaked it on, because once or twice there looked as if there might be some trouble from some folks still mad over losing the war, and thinking we colored men was eyeing their wives a little too closely. I eyed a few, I admit. A good-looking woman doesn't escape my eye, no matter their color or mode of dress or undress. I like to look at mountains too, but that doesn't mean I intend to climb all of them, though I have climbed a few.

When I was dressed, I took the short walk over to the Big Sandy Switch station, leaving my car in the shed with the double doors closed and padlocked. That was the other thing the Pullman job did for me. It allowed me to own a not so bad home in a pretty good spot on the edge of the colored section of town, not too far from the railroad tracks. Some nights I would awake to the rumble of a train, the sound of it on the tracks and its whistle blowing. I had become so accustomed to working on trains, the sounds sometimes made me think I was on board, and I would awake thinking I had work to do.

When I finished my walk and was on board my train, doing my duties, one of the fellows that served lunch got behind, and they called on me to do some of that, though that wasn't my regular job.

I finished up helping, and walked along making my regular rounds, giving passengers this and that, though at least it was early enough I didn't have to deal with settling folks in for the night, which always meant the bell at their sleeping stations would be ringing constantly, wanting me to come and bring them some water, or a different pillow, a fresh, brown blanket, or what have you. Some passengers rang that bell to fetch you and give you jobs out of boredom. They were always the worst tippers.

But this day was all right. We switched over at Tyler and ended up being on the tracks for a while as cotton was loaded on the box cars behind the passenger coaches, and then we headed on toward Fort Worth. It was about three in the afternoon when we came rolling in, and as usual, the cow shit greeted us well before the station.

We hadn't no more than settled in, then a couple of young men boarded, one of them with cheeks so rosy they looked to have been pinched. He was well dressed and had a nice white hat with a narrow brim. He looked at me, and that sweet face didn't go with the eyes, which were light blue and cold as ice in a dead man's ass.

He studied me, then walked toward the front of the train while the other sat in my section. The one in my section looked like he had been in a fight with a grizzly bear and lost. I hadn't never seen a man that ugly by either nature or accident. It was like his face had a hobby of collecting scars and wounds. His tan narrow-brimmed hat was bent up in front, and he wore dark clothes that were moth-eaten and patched, held together mostly by body odor that reminded me of rotten persimmons in a coffee can. His gray coat was a size too big, as if he had bought it with the intention of growing fat.

He was looking around quite a bit, and after we got to rolling, I could see he was nervous as a goat at a Texas barbecue. He lit a cheap cigar and stunk up the place, and the smoke from his stogie filled the passenger car and blended with that from other smokers that were puffing on less foul-smelling tobaccos. Windows were open all along the car, and the smoke was slowly curling out of them.

I collected tickets, and went on about my duties. At the front of my car a couple were sitting by each other in a seat near the door to the next passenger car, and they looked dressy for my section, as if they had become too tired to make the trek to the first-class car. The man had a fat, brown mustache and was quite handsome, wore an expensive wool suit. He had a little brown hat that looked as if it belonged on a leprechaun situated on his knee. The woman was so gorgeous as to give me eye strain; red hair, blue dress, black button-up shoes that made me long to unbutton them. I tried not to stare at her, and when I took their tickets, they both smiled at me and spoke politely.

Short time later the man with the scarred face and the rotten persimmon smell, called me over. "Hey, Georgie-boy. Get me some coffee."

Of course, my first thought was to snap his neck, but I had that thought often, as certain passengers felt it their duty to try and make themselves more important than they were by making everyone else less important, especially us porters.

"No coffee, sir, until they make a fresh batch, which will be an hour or so."

This answer required considerable concentration on his part. He flicked his stogie out the open window, looked up at me as if I were a tree he was considering for fire wood, said, "I won't want any then."

"Sorry, sir."

"Why don't you go make me some?"

"That's not part of my duties. They make it, I can bring it, but where you're sitting, there's no place to set the coffee. You got to be riding a different level of car."

"So, you work the poor man's car?"

"I work several cars, sir, but today I work in the one you can afford to ride."

He let those words chew around in his head a bit, and I don't think he digested them enough to know if I insulted him or not. As he was still working on that, I moved on down the line.

It wasn't much longer after that, than the train was brought to a quick stop, flinging me and the passengers around. I should have known something was up, because of how nervous the loud mouth had been, and the way he had braced himself before the stop.

I got up off the floor, and there standing in the aisle with a pistol he had drawn from under his coat, was the ugly bastard, grinning tobacco-colored teeth at me. He started yelling, commanding me to step into a place between seats, and he went down the aisle taking wallets, change, rings and necklaces and such from everyone, dropping them into a sack he had pulled out from under that oversized coat.

He pointed his gun at me, and said, "What you got?"

"Just the time of day, sir."

"Yeah, well, I reckon I believe you." He moved down to another row, said, "But you," and now he was gesturing toward a young woman no more than sixteen in my view. "Pull that necklace and ring off, and while you're at it, maybe I ought to take your panties to smell on my way riding out of town. I could put 'em over my head and feel real good about it."

He didn't insist on the panties, but he did take her jewelry. Out the window then, I saw there was six horses showing up, two of them without riders, being led by the others. There was a couple of young, white fellows who looked like they had been snatched out of grade school and given guns. Like the dung heap in our car, none of them had bothered to wear masks to hide their features.

One had big apple cheeks, beaming red, and he was a match for the man who had come aboard at Fort Worth, the bright cheek fellow with the dead cold eyes. His black range hat was tilted back and I could see a sheaf of blond hair poking out from under it. He had one of those new auto-pistols on his hip. He looked like someone who ought to be preaching a sermon instead of robbing a train. I knew right then they were what the papers labeled the Radiant Apple gang, referring to the color of the gang's leaders and their cheeks. They didn't look all that much alike, except for that peculiar hereditary pass down of luminous cheeks, but that trait damn sure branded them.

They were low level bandits that wanted to be Jesse James, but were more like headless chickens that could shoot revolvers. They usually worked grocery stores and banks in small towns, robbed people on the road. Now they were moving up to trains. They hadn't even picked one carrying a payroll. They were completely low rent.

The other two horses had colored boys on their backs, one of them a big strong man in a plaid shirt and black hat, and I recognized the other right off. He was mounted on a beautiful white and chestnut paint horse that couldn't stop pawing the ground. He was lean and sat tall in the saddle. He had a hat I had given him some years back. It had been battered by the rain and the wind, and was no longer white, but was gray and speckled with time and stain.

Riding the paint was my son, Rufus. I can't tell you what the paint's name was.

—⟋⟍—

THERE was starting to be a bit of panic in the aisles, and I said, "Everyone remain calm until this gentleman and his companions finish their business, and then we'll all go home safe and sound and without bullet wounds."

Stinky-Big-Coat looked at me and smiled his stained teeth. "Listen to coon boy here, and everything will be all right. Just fine."

He was still working his way down the row with his sack, collecting items. One man protested and ended up being banged across the head with the barrel of the pistol, causing him to slump and put a hand to the top of his head. He used his other hand to come up with his wallet and a silver pin he pulled right off his tie.

Calm as I was acting, my stomach was churning to see my son out there. The colored fellow in the plaid shirt was left to hold the horses, and now the other bunch were on board, including Rufus. They had put their two plants on board, and now that the train had been forced to stop, most likely due to Stinky-Big-Coat's partner punching a pistol in the engineer's ear, the others had joined them at the allotted spot, going through the cars, gathering loot.

I thought that not only had Rufus taken the wrong trail, but it looked as if he had made that trail his home.

I felt sad and weak and disappointed. I was also mad as a whole nest of disturbed hornets.

Rufus came into the car then carrying a white bag for loot. He stood at the far end near the door and watched me. He looked so much like my young self, including the big ears, that I felt as if I were looking in a mirror when I was twenty-one. He had his gun drawn, a nice new Colt revolver.

He had seen me from outside, and I knew he was surprised, because it wasn't my regular shift. He looked at me and his face had a melting look, like he was facing heated air blowing out of Hell's doorway.

Stinky-Big-Coat was starting to get more worked up, and when Rufus came in, he said, "Took you long enough."

"I'm on time," Rufus said, not looking at him, but looking at me. I'm sure he could feel my disappointment floating across the passenger car.

Rufus was standing nearby as Stinky-Big-Coat started harassing the attractive, polite couple that I thought looked as if they were in the wrong coach. He was wanting her wedding ring, which she was reluctant to part with. Her husband, the one with the dark mustache, stood up from his seat, said, "Listen here. That's too far."

Stinky-Big-Coat lifted his pistol and standing no more than a foot apart, shot the man in the chest. It was a killing shot, and the man fell on the floor between seats, on top of his wife's feet. She shrieked like an eagle.

"That wasn't needed," Rufus said.

The woman wailed. Stinky-Big-Coat stuck the pistol at her. "Give me that goddamn ring."

She started struggling to get her ring off, crying all the while.

"I'll cut that finger off, you don't give me that ring."

She continued to struggle. Stinky-Big-Coat whacked her slightly across the forehead with the pistol. Causing her to turn sideways in her seat and touch her forehead. Her fingers specked red.

Rufus struck out, hit Stinky-Big-Coat upside the head with his own pistol, bringing him to one knee. "You stupid bastard. Leave it."

"You can't do that to me," Stinky-Big-Coat said.

"Just did," Rufus said. "Keep the ring, lady. Sorry about your husband. Come on. That's enough. Let's go."

"Sorry," she said. "You're sorry?"

Rufus swallowed and almost said something. Then he glanced at me, wheeled and went swiftly back the way he had come, through the connecting passenger car, letting the door shut behind him.

Stinky-Big-Coat wobbled to his feet. "He ain't no boss of me. Give me that ring."

He wasn't paying attention to me anymore. As he was grabbing the crying lady's hand, trying to pull the ring off it, I reached back and pulled my derringer and held it against the side of my leg and started out from between the seats and down the aisle.

Stinky-Big-Coat noted me then, turned at me with his pistol, his brown teeth showing, excitement burning in his eyes like dry leaves on fire. Here was his opportunity to prove again what a big-time killer he was.

Only thing that foiled that plan was I shot him right between the eyes. I was still quick and damn near a dead shot. Although, at that distance, a blind man with the trembles might have managed the same.

The shot jerked Stinky's head and his hat flew off. He went to his knees and settled there a moment with his mouth open, then fell forward in the aisle on his face, his teeth taking the brunt of it, hard enough one flew out of his mouth and slid under one of the seats.

I HAD ANOTHER LOAD in the derringer. I stepped through the passenger car, and into the next one, taking the same route my son had, ready for anything, fearing a confrontation between Rufus and myself.

There were only the passengers in there. The robbers had come and gone, quick as starving squirrels grabbing acorns.

I leaned between a row of seats and passengers, looked out the window. I saw the men loading up on their horses, letting the one riderless horse loose. The apple-cheeked man I had seen go up front before was now mounted. He eyed me, and for a moment I thought he might take a shot at me through the window. Even from that distance, those blue ice eyes were chilly. I shouted for all the passengers to get down. It was a command from a porter, but they responded.

My son was looking at my face in the window. He studied me for a long moment, whirled his horse about, and him and his bunch took off across the field like they were cats with their tails on fire. Soon they were dots in the distance, riding those horses for all they would give.

I slipped the derringer back under my jacket. Everyone started talking at once. It took a while before the train began moving again. I went back to my car and covered up the dead man's body with a blanket. I made sure to use a brown one, so as no white folk would be ass-twitched over me giving him a blue one, the ones reserved for the negroes. Even in death, a white fella's folks might find a peeve with a blanket a negro might have been under being placed over a white man, even if he was a robber and a murderer.

I told the woman whose ring Stinky-Big-Coat had tried to take, "Sorry for your loss, ma'am," which is a useless sympathy, and no matter how you present it, always sounds false.

She grabbed my arm. "Thank you, George. Thank you."

"Yes, ma'am."

"Your real name?"

"Nat Love, ma'am."

"Mrs. Charlie Chumley... The late Mrs. Charlie Chumley. Oh, what do I do now?"

"I can't say, ma'am. I'll get a blanket for your husband." I had only had the one in the overhead, and I would have to go back to another car to get another.

I did that, choosing the proper color, and came back and covered him gently and picked up his little hat that had fallen off his knee when he had stood up.

After that, I went on about my business, trying to make the rest of the ride as common as possible, and believe me, it wasn't possible. I gave out free drinks, and not the soft kind, violating policy. That stuff was meant for the first-class cars, but it seemed the right time and place for it. Most everyone accepted. For a long time, it was quiet, and then everyone was talking at once, and that poor Mrs. Chumley had begun to shake along with her crying.

I got another blanket and draped it over her shoulders. I knew the chill was not from the air but from the horror, but I thought it might make her feel some comfort, as if in the womb.

When I could manage, I found a place in the baggage section and sat down on a steamer trunk. I held my hand out in front of me. Steady as a rock. My time in the Old West had kept me in control of my wits and muscles. I tried to remember when I had shot Stinky-Big-Coat, but all I remembered was removing the gun from under my coat and the next thing I knew he was dead.

I took a couple deep breaths, and went back to my work. It seemed like it took forever for the train to turn around on switch tracks and carry us back to Fort Worth. I could feel every rumble and rattle beneath my feet, as if for the first time. I wanted to get off that car, off that train. I was actually looking forward to the stench of cow shit.

THE LAW AND the Pullman Company in Fort Worth put me up in a barn, which was nice enough if you didn't mind sitting on a turned over milk bucket watching chickens cackle and a milk cow moo. There were rats too, and they were frisky and brave and would come sniff at the toes of my shoes. A couple of amorous and not at all shy rats were screwing for all it was worth not five feet from where I sat. The male rat was energetic and the female rat looked as if she couldn't wait for it to be over with so she might roll a cigarette.

The law had me sitting there for quite a while. They had got to me when I came off the train, information having already been wired ahead by telegram.

The fellow that came in to see me was a skinny man with a nose like a pickle and a brown suit like a cheap tent. He had pock scars on his face and his string tie was limp. He had a paper bag under his arm. He looked like the thought of life made him tired. He sized me up. I stood up from my bucket, put my hands behind my back, held them together.

After looking me over, he said, "I work for the railroad. I'm a railway detective. Name is Buck Simms."

"Yes, sir."

"You shot that man twixt the eyes, didn't you?"

"Yes, sir."

"Damn good shot, are you?"

"I was lucky. We were close."

"Uh-huh. Not supposed to have a gun on you, being a colored and all."

"Yes, sir."

"There's them don't like a colored man shooting a white man."

"Didn't seem to have any choice."

"No. No, you didn't. Mrs. Chumley said you saved her life. We'll forget the gun. She says you were cool and calm and well collected."

"I have been under some stress before," I said.

"You know any of them men?"

Now was the moment of truth, and I lied. "No, sir."

"All right then. We ain't going to do nothing to you. But you might can do something for us."

"What would that be, sir?"

"Let me make sure of something first," he said, and removed two old Dime novels from the paper bag. He pushed them toward me. "This you?"

I took them. They were DEADWOOD DICK novels.

"In a manner of speaking."

"You're white in them books, but I was told they are about you."

"They snookered on me," I said.

"Yeah?"

"Yes, sir."

"How was you snookered?"

"No man, white, black, or any other color, could do the things they have me doing. But they are built on a brief reputation I had as a crack shot and a territorial marshal for Judge Parker. I changed colors between my real life and the page."

"I was told about you by one of the other porters."

"That would be Sam Dritt," I said. We all knew Sam Dritt as Blabbermouth, for the obvious reason. I hadn't even known he was on the train that day, my shift being different and all. Perhaps he had been at the Fort Worth station.

"He rushed in to tell us that right way."

"Did he, sir?"

"Said you could track a rat fart through blackberry vines."

"He exaggerated. Fact is, I'm a so-so tracker. Real tracker was a man named Choctaw. He worked with me from time to time. He could track that rat fart through berry vines in a high wind with one nostril stuffed full of dirty leaves."

"Then maybe it's him we need?"

"Could be, sir." But already I was beginning to see a possible plan to find my son and cease his ride down the wrong trail. "Thing is, Choctaw is a hell of a tracker, but I'm the detective, so to speak. He can smell the rats out, but I'm the one that can find the little farters, trap them and bring them in."

I was, of course, exaggerating my detective skills. I had been a man hunter, a bounty hunter with a badge.

Buck noticed the rats in the corner. They were resting after their amorous activity. The male was heaving hard. "I could track them rats."

"Yes, sir."

He turned and studied me for a long moment. "You're a black one, aren't you?"

I said nothing.

"You have to bring them in?" Buck said.

"What are you suggesting, sir."

"I'm saying this out of time Radiant Apple gang, as they're being called. Goddamn newspapers. Are dangerous and think they're the James-Youngers. The Jameses and Youngers had smarter horses than this bunch, but they have done killed someone they shouldn't. Of course, anyone being killed isn't good, but them with money winging their way to hell or heaven, well, that's a goddamn tragedy. Mrs. Charlene Chumley is a rich widow and her husband was a major investor in the Pullman cars that the train leases. I think that's how it works."

"Close sir. Pullman company owns the cars, and we porters, cooks, that sort of thing, work for that company. But Pullman don't own the train. Railroad and Pullman work together. You might call it a joint venture."

I thought this was stuff a railroad detective should know, but I had a feeling they had just picked Buck off a shelf for the job.

"You've had some education?" Buck said.

"Not in a formal manner. But if you want me to hunt these men and bring them in, or shoot them dead if the situation deserves it, then I'm your man."

"Mrs. Chumley, when she heard about your past, she insisted on you.

"May I ask why the Chumleys were riding in the common passenger section?"

"They wanted to sit in a passenger car to know what they were helping finance as investors."

"I see."

"You look fit. How old are you?"

I told him.

"Hell, you look fitter than me, and I'm ten years less your age."

I didn't argue with this.

"I want you to hunt them down and make sure they're no longer trouble. Is that understood."

"I would attempt to bring them in alive. I'm not a killer by choice. But if it comes to it, I won't waffle."

"If they should wind up dead, no tears will be shed here. Fact is, that might make me look so good setting this up, that I could be chosen by Mrs. Chumley to shit a pile on their graves in place of a tombstone. Things go bad, then you and me both look bad. That might mean your job is a bit more unlikely when you come home. I might lose mine as well. I wouldn't like that."

"Why put someone like me on it when there's law enforcement?"

"Trains have lately been robbed five times, simple stuff, but there have been two deaths. Last time it was one of the Radiant Apple boys done the killing. Little boy, ten, I think, wouldn't shut up, kept blowing a god-damn whistle. Was excited and nervous you see, way kids are. Got my own kids, little bastards. I can kind of see why someone would want to shoot the little scamp, but then again, be a lot less kids if we all responded to our natural desire to make them shut the hell up for a while. Thing is, those Radiant Apple boys are meaner than they look. They have hit a few banks, as well as trains, and robbed a dry goods store in Amarillo, took off with some money, bottles of sarsaparilla, and gum ball candy. Licorice, I think. They beat the clerk some and fondled his wife, but didn't kill or ruin her womanhood. I think they may have beat him because the gum balls were licorice. Who the fuck makes licorice gum balls?"

I was beginning to suspect Buck had once upon a time had a less than favorable experience with licorice and held a grudge.

He told me then a lot about the gang that I already knew from reading the papers.

"They have never stolen big money, but they are a nuisance and have killed folks. Pullman Company. Rail lines. Couple of banks. They all want to put an end to the gang before people start fearing to ride the trains or tuck their money in banks. Law enforcement, so far, couldn't find their dicks with both hands and don't know a tick on their balls from a blessing from God. They need someone on it full time that's got the old-time experience of riding the range, going without a bath and eating grit in their food, dealing with the elements. Elements means rain and wind and heat and such. I used to could do it, but it don't appeal to me no more. It gets about six p.m., I'm ready to go home and lie in bed and hope my wife don't have a headache and the lumbago. Thing is, my job as a railroad detective doesn't include me doing what you can do better. So, straight to it. How much will you do it for, this finding them?"

"Well, sir. I'm glad to do it, but it may take a while. And I'd like for you to hire on Choctaw as my tracker, though it might take me a few days to rustle him up. I have crossed a few letters with him, but haven't seen him in years."

"All right, but you still haven't named the price you'd do it for."

"Would you care to make a suggestion?"

He did.

"No, sir. That is far too little for a chance to be killed, and that can't include Choctaw, too, and I need him to do it right and quick."

"Get too pushy here, I can get a white man to do the job."

"For a bigger price, because he is white. And I doubt he'll have had my experience. Also, Mrs. Chumley asked for me specifically, did she not?"

Buck considered on that for so long, I thought he might have died standing up.

"All right then. I'll double the offer. Mrs. Chumley said she'd pay half out of her own pocket, Pullman will pay some, the railroad will pay a patch. The banks. That work for you?"

"That doesn't include Choctaw's pay, which needs to be at least as much as you were first offering me, plus expenses."

"I'm not used to negotiating terms with a colored."

I didn't say anything.

"Hell, not my money. All right. I'll tell Mrs. Chumley, Pullman, the railroad, and the banks the deal. I don't think there will be any disagreement over those terms."

"And sir, if you pardon, not to disparage my confidence in you as my employer, I need all of that agreement, including the part that contains the fee, expenses, and the price for Choctaw, in writing. And notarized."

"You are one uppity colored."

"No, sir. Just specific about what I'm signing on for, as it could lead to a coyote sucking on my bones."

"You want that there agreement on blue paper, or maybe a nice pink pastel?"

"No, sir. Nice as that would be, common white paper will be sufficient, though if I had my druthers, I am partial to a soft olive green."

T HEY GAVE ME the signed contract and an allowance to get started, as well as some written information on the gang, and a stack of newspapers where they were mentioned, so I might brush up on them and maybe glean an idea or two about how to go after them.

I thought maybe I needed new weapons, but instead decided to take out my old oak handle Peacemaker, 1892 revolver, and give it a once-over. That handle had been put on for me special after mine had been shattered by a bullet that just missed blowing my hand off. Happened while I was reaching for it in my holster. Had I been a moment quicker, my fingers would have been in place for snipping, and I wouldn't have had to roll off my horse and pull my other pistol and dot my would-be killer a couple of times. Though, I got to be honest and tell I shot four shots, two that missed, and two that hit. The ones that hit, they're the ones that counted.

I had been good about keeping that pistol clean for years, so except for a touch-up and ammunition I would need to buy, I decided on it as my main weapon. There was a black, soft cowhide holster that went with it, simple and cut so that the gun could be tied against my thigh. The holster was the sort you could pull from quickly without snagging.

I still had my old LeMat revolver, but decided to let it stay packed away, feeling it might be a bit dated and less dependable, having been used severely in the past, and taken less care of by me. It was nine shot with a shotgun shell as well, and was rare. I thought about that shotgun shell surprise and regretted leaving it home a little, but decided to substitute with a Winchester Model 1912 pump shotgun I traded for in the year of its birth. I had only used it a few times to provide quail and dove for the table. I had a strap attached to it to make it an easier tote. I also had a Winchester 93 rifle from my last riding days, and it was serviceable enough, me needing only to buy some ammunition for it. Lastly, as a backup gun I decided on my holstered Smith and Wesson pistol I had bought in 1910. A .44 caliber shooter with gold-plated ivory grips. I had never used it.

As final backup, I had my derringer, of course. Having my own guns instead of buying new ones left me with more money to keep from the allowance.

My next step was to find Choctaw.

I dug out his old letters and discovered he had nested last in Oklahoma, up in what had once been known as the Nations. He had taken up with a Creek lady he called Little Wind, which was not her name, but was a fart joke. According to his letters, she liked beans.

That's all I had to go on, and a certain feeling that Oklahoma was the direction the Radiant Apple gang had gone, due to their leaders, the Albrights, had come from there, and seemed to circulate back after crime sprees. From the notes and papers I was given, I made some deductions. They were not known for great dedication to their craft, as their robberies were random, and the only two in the gang that remained consistent were the two apple cheek brothers, Charlie and Lowe Albright. Charlie was thought to be the main leader, and despite their somewhat cherubic appearance, both were said to be impulsive, explosively mean, and by all accounts, indifferent shots.

Charlie and his brother Lowe carried automatic pistols and the story was they had a fast-firing military weapon they had used on only one known occasion, and their targets had been cattle in a pasture, and the killing of the cattle with the weapon had been done for fun, not profit. They just wanted to see something die. Or so went the story. I hoped it wasn't true for the cows' sake, and for any future encounter I might have with them. I was also relieved to see this cow shooting had taken place at a time I knew Rufus couldn't have been with them.

Day of the train robbery they hadn't had such a weapon. The train robbery was in my view a quick pickup of dough to head north to Oklahoma, and the robbery hadn't gone as smooth as they expected. Well, it hadn't for Mr. Chumley and Stinky-Old-Coat anyway. I doubt the gang had a little get-together in Stinky's memory later that day. He was to them most likely about as inspiring as an empty cartridge. You could at least reload one of them, but Stinky-Old-Coat couldn't be reloaded with anything other than embalming fluid.

I figured the Albright boys took in people like my son, lost souls looking for a perch to light on, or numbskulls with the native intelligence of a dog turd. This way they could be sure to stay in control. I hoped Rufus wasn't in too deep with them. He had at least defended poor Mrs. Chumley before I had to shoot ole Stinky and send him sailing on the River Styx without so much as a travel coin.

I finished up my thoughts on the gang, gathered some goods and drove into town.

I had to go through the back door to the general store, but I showed my allowance papers to the owner and credited some supplies and ammunition to the railroad detective, or rather to the charge account he had set up for me. I doubled the dry goods, as Choctaw could eat like a mountain lion, and how long we might be on the road was undetermined. I got myself a sarsaparilla and a peppermint stick and put it on the bill just for me for having to go through the back door.

I bought me some extra gas in sturdy glass jugs, and put them in the floorboard of the backseat wrapped in thick towels. I put all the goods and weapons and ammunition on the backseat, and covered them with a blanket. I marked up a map, started the Ford up, working the high-low pedal and the gears off the steering wheel, and away I rolled.

It crossed my mind to stop by Lillian's place, see if I could talk to her, but she might have a customer, and that would only embarrass the both of us. I decided I had made my choice, and it was time to move on. I didn't completely believe that, but I told myself I did.

It was a long way to Oklahoma with the road bouncing my ass up and down, but I stayed steady, and bought gas when I could find a place to do so. Some places didn't sell to coloreds, but there was generally a filling station of sorts, or some place in colored sections along the way where I could freshen up my gas in the tank and in the jugs.

I took my time on that trip, enjoying the freedom from the rail cars and feeling about ten years younger. I thought about my son a lot. I wasn't sure how that was going to work out, but I had some fear I might have a bullet-to-bullet confrontation with him, and I damn sure didn't want that. I thought about Lillian too. Maybe I did love her enough. It might not be the same as with my wife, but it was something. It might be good for both of us. Maybe when I got back, if I got back, I'd see how the both of us felt on the matter.

When I got up to Eastern Oklahoma and the town of Hooty Hoot, where Choctaw was said to live, where he kept a General Delivery address, I went over to the post office to see if anyone might know where he hung his hat.

I had to stand in the colored line for about forty-five minutes, as the two clerks let the white customers go first, and though I moved up in line, when white folks came in, the colored waiting line was abandoned, and stayed that way until white customers diminished. I found the whole thing wearing and humiliating. There was an old colored man mopping over in one corner, and it must have been a dirty corner, because he didn't budge from it. That spot would soon shine like a fresh-minted silver dollar.

When I got up to the window, I told the heavy lady with the bunched up hair sitting behind it, that I was working for Pullman and the railroad and showed her my papers. If she was impressed, she held it back from viewing. I asked about Choctaw, if she knew him and if he had a time when he picked up his mail. She surprised me by knowing exactly who I was talking about. She said, "Ain't he part colored?"

"I don't know, ma'am. I know he's got Indian in him. Hence the name."

He was colored, as well as part Indian, but I figured they liked Indians slightly better. Every white person had started claiming to have Indian blood, always from some Cherokee or Comanche princess or war chief, or such, when most of them were as Irish as a shamrock. Wasn't nobody making a parade of having colored blood, though. One drop of that and you were at the back of any line and short on possibilities.

"A woman comes in to collect the mail for him on Wednesday."

It was Tuesday.

"He never gets much mail, save for a letter or two now and then, so mostly she comes in and goes out with empty hands, but she nearly always comes in. Cute little trick. Indian gal. I don't think they're legally married, and I hate to see that kind of sinning, don't you?"

"Can't sleep at night thinking about it," and wondered if she might actually be up for a little sin if she got the chance.

I asked if she knew where Choctaw and the cute little trick lived. She did not.

I started out. The old man with the mop looked up and lifted his head in summons. I went over to him, careful not to stand in the spot where he was working.

"That Choctaw. He lives up on Blackberry Hill. It's about five miles south of here."

"Thank you."

"Don't know me, do you Deadwood?"

I studied him, trying to recall him, but I didn't.

"You served a warrant on me back in the day."

"I don't remember."

"Tom Miller. I stole some chickens. You gave me the money for the fine."

"Did I?"

"You did. I stole them chickens because our family was hungry. Shouldn't ought to, but I did. I ain't forgot what you did for me, talking to the judge way you did, so as he let me go with that the fine paid. You let him think I paid it, anyway. I ain't forgot."

"I have."

"But I haven't. You be careful whatever you're doing."

"You wouldn't have any idea where them they call the Radiant Apple gang hangs their hats, would you?"

"Them two Albright boys is bad news, I tell you that. But all I know is up in the hills, when they ain't into mischief. They got family and friends in this town. They could screw a donkey and call it Mildred, and there's those would invite them and their donkey to church. Let Mildred be baptized. So, you keep your head up and your hands near your shooters. Though I don't see you got none."

"I got some."

"Good. You'll need 'em. And I was you, I'd keep them close from here on out, if you're looking for them boys. They ain't smart, but they're mean."

—⁓—

BLACKBERRY Hill was well named. It was a large sandy hill that climbed up into some pecan trees, but before the trees, on either side of a couple of tire tracks, was a mass of twisting blackberry vines. Come spring, it would be like bear heaven, and I didn't blame them bears. Nothing better than eating a mess of ripe blackberries. The vines were also a wonderful place for snakes to hide out in.

I drove to the top of the hill, bounced through a split in a grove of persimmon trees, came to a clearing, and found a well-built log cabin with a rock fireplace and a long porch up front with a wood shingle roof hanging over it. A barn was off to the right, and it was good sized and painted blood-red and appeared well-tended. Chickens were roaming about, and there was a shadow moving over them. A hawk, looking for a chicken supper.

There was a rock well curb in front of the house with a little roof over it, and a support post for a bucket, rope, and crank. Between house and barn, a Ford truck was parked with slat boards on either side of the bed. There were fields of corn beyond the barn, and off to the left of the house. It all looked like some kind of painting. Choctaw had done all right.

I parked in the yard, and was climbing out of the car, when a dark-haired woman about the size of a leprechaun standing on a stool came out of the house and let the screen door slam behind her. She had a double barrel shotgun with her. It was long barreled and looked to be a ten gauge. It was taller than she was. She pointed it at me, bracing the stock against her hip.

"Stay right there in that car, or I'll blow the knees out from under you."

SHE MIGHT MANAGE to cut me off at the knees, but big
a gauge as that gun was, she had a good chance of
knocking her own leg off from the recoil.

The screen door squeaked and a man came out and
settled the door gently into place, looked out at me. It
was Choctaw. He was still long and lanky, though he
had put on a few pounds, and his skin seemed a little
darker than I remembered, but still had a reddish cast.
Domestic life agreed with him, I figured.

"Ah, honey, you don't have to shoot him, that's Nat
Love. Me and him have ridden many a mile together."

"Don't care," she said.

"We're friends, Little Wind."

"Goddamn friends," she said.

"Put the shotgun down, dear."

Little Wind lowered the shotgun, but I didn't rush up to the porch. She still had her eyes on me. She was a pretty thing, but she damn near had smoke coming out of her nose.

"She's a little hot-headed. Probably thinks you're a shoe salesman, or some such. You ain't, are you?"

"I have dipped low in life," I said, "but I am not a door-to-door salesman. If I were, if asked my job, I'd tell them I dug latrines before admitting to the other."

"That's a good thing. Come on up, Nat."

"You stay there," Little Wind said.

"Her bark's worse than her bite," Choctaw said.

"It's the shotgun's bite I'm worried about."

"Naw, it's all right. Give me the gun, sweetie."

She gave it up, but she didn't look happy about it. Choctaw unloaded the shotgun and put the shells in his shirt pocket.

—⚏—

"I don't like you," Little Wind said, as I came up on the porch.

"You don't know me."

"She don't like nobody much," Choctaw said. "I think she likes me some."

"Don't be too sure," she said.

"She's extra pissy today. Bobcat got in our chickens last night, killed four or five. I tracked him this morning and found his tree, but couldn't bring myself to kill him. He was just doing what a bobcat does."

We went inside as Little Wind said, "He don't kill nothing. Won't step on roaches."

Choctaw leaned the shotgun against the door frame. "I've gotten real peaceful in my old age," he said.

"Would you shoot a man?"

"Sooner than a bobcat."

"Would you track again and shoot one if you got in tight spot and had to?"

"Sooner than a bobcat."

"Would you help me track some men?"

"I don't know, Nat. I mean, I got the farm here."

"We hire work done," Little Wind said. By this time we had all gotten seated at the dining table. "He stays home. I have money because I got oil."

"She's Osage. Found oil on their lands, and bunches of them are rich. We got a show farm, Nat. We hire white people to keep it up."

"That's funny," I said.

"Ain't it."

"He's not going anywhere." She laid some heavy eyeballs on me then, and her pretty little mouth dipped at the corners.

"I'm just here to ask," I said. "I have what you might call a temporary railroad detective badge and papers, and I got warrants on the Radiant Apple gang."

"Those assholes. They're no more real bandits than that chicken-killing bobcat, except they ain't got the morals. In our day, we'd have sent out one of the children and a pet chicken to bring them in. Course, I don't have any children, though I do have the chickens."

"My chickens," Little Wind said.

I thought I might not ought to mention the hawk right then, lest I stir her up and have her load the shotgun again. I didn't want her weaponized.

"Children is part of this, Choctaw. My son is with them."

"Oh."

"He helped rob a train in Fort Worth when I was working. A man was killed. Wasn't him done it, and he tried to stop the man from going on with his spree. Way it turned out I shot the bandit between the eyes with a derringer. I don't even know his name."

"Goddamn, Nat. You're still a rowdy."

"He was about to shoot a woman named Chumley. Her husband was the one this unnamed outlaw killed, and he was threating the woman, and I had to shoot him. It was him or me or maybe her."

"I know that's true. You ain't an indiscriminate shooter."

"He ain't going," Little Wind said to me, her eyes more narrow now, the corners of her lips dipping deeper.

"The pay is tremendous for the times," I said. "We also got running money. Supplies and horse money and such. Car of mine won't do much for us where we need to go."

"Too bad you ain't got Ole Satan," he said.

He was referring to a black horse I once had. Mean as a scorpion and one hell of a cayuse, gone on to the great corral in the sky, still bucking would be my guess. I ate part of him, but that's a different story.

"No. I don't have Satan. But I got the documents and the money to get what we need. Railroad is supplying me, along with the Pullman company."

"Quite a bit different than being a porter."

"I know this job better, Choctaw, and so do you."

"He don't need money," Little Wind said.

"I need to think on it," Choctaw said.

"You're not going," Little Wind said.

"Stay for supper, Nat. Bed down, and I'll tell you in the morning."

"You're not going. You go, don't come back."

"She knows her mind," Choctaw said.

Little Wind latched her gaze on me again, and this time I could feel it all the way through my head and onto the back of my neck.

"He's not going."

—⚏—

THAT night after a supper of beans and some heavy pan-fried bread that really suited my stomach right, all of it cooked by Choctaw, me and him sat out on the porch. Little Wind sat out behind some bushes near the chicken coop. She was waiting on that bobcat.

"She is the goddamndest killer of things," Choctaw said. "She ain't much of shot, though. Why she has the shotgun. Even there she might miss."

Choctaw was smoking his pipe and rocking. I was in another rocking chair set out to the side of him so I could look at him in the dark. I could see his shape and a cloud of smoke rising up from him.

"How'd you come to be here, Choctaw? Got to say, Little Wind is right. You don't need to go out in the wilds. She's young and you got money and you got land and you got white people plowing and such for you. Truth is, we may both have been too long from the rough, and might not make our way the way we remember, if we even remember right."

"We remember right. You and me, we had some times together."

"You know I went down to East Texas and made a job as a porter, but you never said in your letters what you were doing, until you mentioned Little Wind and living here in Oklahoma."

"Still think of it as the territories. Hard to fathom it part of the United States of America. Seems like only yesterday you and me was tracking human varmints through these lands. I didn't mention what I was doing in those letters, because I'm not really doing anything."

"I'm on a varmint hunt."

"What about your son?"

"I don't know the answer to that yet, but I suppose I got to bring him in."

"You stick to the law a little too tight, Nat. Sometimes you got to bend it."

"Rufus broke it. He broke it with them others."

"But he didn't kill nobody."

"That I know of."

"Well, Nat, to get back to your question about what I been doing. I become a bit of a whisky runner to the Indians who couldn't buy it legal, and I was helping make a bunch of drunk and lousy feeling Indians, so I quit that. Then I went to being a bounty hunter for awhile, which ain't far off what we did when I tracked with you for the marshals.

"I was trailing this fellow who had killed his entire family with an axe on account of his flapjacks was short on the amount of s'urp he liked on them, and it just set him off. Except for taking that axe to some of the livestock now and then, no one had thought of him as dangerous. But whatever was in his head that wasn't set right, tilted completely. He took that axe and set to work on his wife and two boys, the oldest was about ten, and the youngest eight, I think. Well, the youngest was a swift little scamp, and he give his daddy a merry chase, running through some brush and up and down hills. He hid out in a hog wallow in that brush, and would have gotten away, had he not had to cough. And there you have it. Daddy come down on him and chopped him up meaner than the others on account of how much the old man had to chase him. They said you could have put that boy in a dozen paper bags. The head was all split up too."

"How do they know all that occurred," I said.

"Chopped up family was pretty obvious, but they had me follow the boy's trail and discover him in the hog wallow. It was pretty easy to tell what had gone on.

"Anyway, this fella…I think his name was Simmons, but it's been a bit, so not sure I remember right, he got to just enjoying himself and rode on over with his axe and took some neighbors out and killed a prized mule that was loaned out all across the country for plowing. That was the last straw. He was hunted down and found sleeping in the woods holding the reins of his horse that was standing there waiting for him to wake up. They got him easy. But after two days in jail, they took him out to the privy, these two guards, and there was folks watching this go down from across the street, and damn if Simmons—remember, I'm not sure that was his name—didn't jump on one of them guards and bite his jugular out. Nasty work. Like a goddamn wild dog, he was. The other guard tried to shoot him, but he just shot his dying buddy, which I guess was a blessing, as the old boy was squirting all over the place, they say. Anyway, Simmons got on that fellow before he could shoot again, and beat him down, took his pistol away and whacked him in the head with it. That ole boy recovered, but now he thinks he was born in a town in Ireland, and knew a family of leprechauns that cheated at cards. It's kind of a hard story to follow. He was actually born in Topeka up Kansas way, and the closest he'd been to Ireland is a green shirt. He walks a little funny too.

"So, Simmons stole a horse and saddle and an axe from the livery, and covered in blood, he run off. There was a bounty put on him. I decided I could use the money, and took after him. I knew there were others after him as well, but they was all green as grass, so I figured I had the leg up on them. Learned later one of them pursuers had shot another hunter through the head thinking he was Simmons, though he didn't no more look like Simmons than a rabbit. So you can figure what kind of competition I had.

"Now, I trailed Simmons into the Arbuckles, and on up into some stands of trees. I figured I'd get him in the night, come up on him, arrest him, tie him up good, take him back and pick up my payday. I was dreaming on that one, Nat.

"Always liked the Arbuckle Mountains, all that granite rock and clean water and trees and the air smelling like pines and cedar and blackjacks and such, and I guess my joy on nature led partly to what happened. Also, I hadn't chased a runaway in some time, and though I knew Simmons was as nutty as a squirrel's den, I don't think I took him serious enough, you know.

"I reckon I should have when I found his horse. He had rode that beast to death, and had cut out a piece of it for eating, and he hadn't roasted it none, 'cause there was raw meat lying around from where he had chewed. There was cracked bones where he had sucked out the marrow. That ole boy had chopped that meat out with an axe while that horse was laying there dying, or was already dead. I hope it was the last. Anyway, when I found that mess my butthole damn near tied itself in a knot. I figured right then I was going to have to shoot the old boy, and I was well prepared to do that. I had my old converted Colt .44 and a double barrel twelve gauge I had sawed some barrel off of, and I was anticipating close work. But even then, I wasn't taking him as seriously as I should have, you see. I had grown confident thinking back on mine and your days in the wilds, bringing in ruffians and killers dead or alive, so I contemplated on it a little, and just decided I'd have to be a bit sneakier and creep up on his ass like a snake on a frog.

"Turned out the horse eater and family slayer was sneakier than I was. I was riding up a trail that was a tumble of gravel. It was dead dark, and I had tracked my prey to the top of that rise, or so I predicted, because there was a wisp of a low campfire winding up through the cedars. But I had been diddled, because damn if that bastard hadn't snuck down and around behind me on foot. I didn't even hear him. And you know me. I can hear a mouse fart under a bushel basket at fifty paces.

"But he snuck up on me. And he had that axe, and he come rushing out of the brush on the side of the trail, frightened the horse, and it started slipping on gravel. Even as it was sliding backwards, he axed that poor critter center of the head and knocked it stone dead, sent it sliding backwards spraying horse shit and gravel, knocking me off the horse. Thing was, though, he couldn't get the axe out of the horse's head, and that stubborn bastard wouldn't let go of the axe, so away we went down that hill, that horse flipping backwards, then sliding sideways, and me just ahead of it, and ole Simmons hanging onto that axe handle and flapping in the wind like a sheet on a clothes line.

"Down we went, and the axe handle come loose and he lost grip on it. The horse jammed up on the trail, and me and him come together in a clutch at the bottom of the track, which was narrow and close to the edge of a deep drop-off. Then there was this big shadow blotting

[75]

out the moon, and it was my horse come loose of its jam, and it come a bouncing and rolling down on top of us and pinned us."

"Shit."

"I'll say. Still got a mild hitch in my getalong from it. There we was on a hillside with a horse on us, and I couldn't reach my pistol which was under me and the horse, or pull my rifle which was on the other side of the beast. If the ground hadn't been slanted and dented a bit, we'd have been crushed like peanuts. But now I got Simmons on me. I mean we were two feet apart, and he's grabbing at me, trying to bite me like a wild animal, and I'm poking and punching at him, but it's an awkward position I'm in. I can see up the hill, but Simmons can't. And I see the axe that come out of my horse's head sliding by inches in the gravel, coming our way, and I think, if this bastard doesn't eat me right here and now, maybe I can get the axe if it slides past him. Course it could slide up against him, and he might get hold of it and use it on me. Things was tense, Nat."

"I can imagine."

"The axe might as well have been a bird in the sky, though, as it quit sliding and was out of my reach by twenty feet or so. I could lasso a cloud sooner than I could get my mitts on it. So, there I am, me and him trying to hit each other, and then he pulls a knife from somewhere. Up his sleeve, I think. Little knife, but sharp enough for serious work, and he starts stabbing. I got hold of his wrist, and damn if the horse doesn't start sliding, pushing its way over us, and at the same time kind of pushing us toward the edge of the cliff. It was eat shit and call it grits time.

"I got hold of his wrist with both hands and pulled his hand toward me, and the knife, on account of that, was poking me in the shoulder, cutting into me, but that way, getting him up close, I could bite that pig-fucker. I bit the living dog shit out of him, and one of his fingers come loose of the knife, and I got hold of it with my teeth, and started chewing like a wild dog. He started screaming. That mad look in his eyes went away, and he yelled out something that sounded like I'm coming Sally, which was his wife's name, and I found that odd, and right then my horse shifted again, slid over me, but somehow stayed hooked to Simmons, and I had to let him go. I was down in a little dent in the trail, and that saved me, but the weight of the horse was carrying Simmons toward the edge of the cliff. He grabbed at my pants leg, and got hold, but I shook him free, and just before he went over the cliff, he said, 'I hate you,' and away he and my poor dead horse went. I heard them hit down there. It sounded nasty. Kind of a combination between a rock falling on another rock, mixed with a squishy sound.

"I spat out Simmons's finger, and crawled over to the edge of the cliff and looked down. The horse was on the cliff below, but Simmons had bounced off the cliff and was still alive, hanging onto a limb. I mean that bastard had nine lives, maybe ten.

"I could reach my pistol now that I didn't have a horse on top of me, but didn't turn out that I needed it. The limb started cracking. He looked up at me. His face was calm, or seemed that way from up where I was, then the limb broke off, and away he went. He didn't scream or nothing. Just rode the wind all the way down."

"Did you recover his body?"

"Nah, but I was trusted on that. I had chewed off his finger which had a cheap ring on it, and it could be identified. I put it in my shirt pocket. I was banged up bad. My legs were injured, banged up, as the weight of the horse had hurt them considerable. So much I couldn't walk for a couple of days. I crawled along using the axe to pull myself forward when I needed to. I ate bugs and even some grub worms that first day. I felt feverish I hurt so bad. Before night I crawled up against a cedar tree and put my back against it and sat there with the axe beside me, my pistol in my lap. During the night a panther came up and looked at me. I could see it clear, as the moon was reasonable bright. I put my hand on my pistol. He didn't seem anything but curious, and after studying me a while, went on about his panther business.

"It come a soft rain, and that didn't bother me none. It felt good dripping down through the tree limbs, and by morning the sun was out, and I felt like trying to stand, and could, using the tree to hold me up. Using the axe like a cane, I was able to walk, and though it was a tough day, by the next day the swelling had gone down and I could move better. It took me a week to get out of there, and not having any supplies it was more bugs and grubs for me. I finally did shoot me a possum one early night. I had matches in my pants, and cut a bit of wood and cooked him. I think I damn near ate that whole greasy possum. Well, after that I went mostly hungry for a few days, came to a mountain road and a wagon come by with an old man driving it, and two boys in the back.

"The old man gave me a ride, but I had to pay him a quarter. In the wagon bed, it all come down on me. I lay there exhausted beyond anything I'd ever been, hurting all over, deciding I had grown old when I wasn't looking. I tried telling myself it wasn't age. Just what had happened, having a goddamn horse lying on me and fighting a wild man had worn me down, but I knew better. My time as a manhunter was coming to an end. Besides, wasn't enough people breaking the law like they used to. Criminals had all turned to banking, politics and preaching.

"Them two boys in the wagon bed saw that I had a bad gravel drag wound on my leg. It was pretty ugly. My pants were split open and my skin was poking through raw, and maggots had got into it. The boys used a hay straw apiece to poke them, trying to spear them and pull them out as a kind of entertainment. I couldn't stop them. By then all my juices had run down. I couldn't even wipe a fly away from my face.

"We finally got to town, and I showed the sheriff that finger, and they took me at my word. I got paid. I laid up for a few days thinking, and then when I got well, I met Little Wind. Her real name is Angel, but she can poot up a storm eating beans. And the stink. Something, brother. She is small, but deadly in that department. But, bean-stink or none, I am quite attached to her."

"I wouldn't blame you if you stayed home, Choctaw. You got a good life here. You got your wife. And she seems strong on you not going. That sounded serious, her saying don't come back. She's got money and land. I was in your position, I won't lie, you come asking me to do such a thing, even with the varmints being half-assed and the money decent, I wouldn't go."

"You just then lied," Choctaw said.

{ 7 }

I SLEPT ON THE long porch that night, in a rocking chair, covered with a thick blanket and a pillow behind my head, and it was a great sleep. The way the air was cool in the night and early morning and slightly warming just before light made me feel young and fresh.

I folded up the blanket and took it and the pillow into the house with me and placed them on a chair. I could smell food cooking in the kitchen, bacon and eggs. The smell made me hungry, but I didn't intend to invite myself to breakfast.

I decided to slip on out and drive away, buy or rent a horse in town, put it on the railroad bill, and start on my merry way. Problem was, I didn't know exactly where to go. I'd have to ask about in the mountains, and there was nothing to say they hadn't moved on and were robbing children of candy and baby rattles.

I knew how to look for them, though, and in time, I'd find them.

As I was about to go out, Little Wind appeared from the kitchen. "Come, breakfast is ready."

"Yes ma'am."

I followed her into the kitchen, reaching to remove a hat I wasn't wearing and had left in the car. In the kitchen Choctaw was at the table drinking coffee, and I could see he had a bedroll and few possibles packed up, resting on the floor against a wall. His Winchester poked out of the bedroll and his old white trail hat was on top of it.

I didn't say anything. I sat down where I was told to sit, and then Little Wind sat down. Choctaw got up and went over and put a stick of wood in the stove, and looked down on a huge frying pan of eggs and bacon cooking. He took a spatula and filled three plates, then he grabbed a rag and used it to hold the coffee pot handle and pour us cups of coffee.

"I cook a lot these days," Choctaw said.

"All he's good for," Little Wind said.

There was a big slab of sourdough bread on the table, and Little Wind cut us chunks from it, and we ate breakfast.

When we finished, Choctaw said, "It's cracking light, so let's go."

"Light has already cracked," Little Wind said.

I thanked Little Wind for her hospitality.

"Go fuck yourself," she said.

"Yes ma'am."

"I'll be back," Choctaw said, taking a last sip of coffee.

"Know what I said," Little Wind said.

"Yeah," Choctaw said. "But you don't mean it."

He stopped to pick up his bedroll and sack of possibles, put on his hat. Little Wind stood up, went to him and hugged him. He dropped his goods and they kissed.

Not to make it embarrassing, I went out on the porch and watched solid sunlight begin to melt the darkness. It looked like someone had dropped a big strawberry in a pit of ink, the way the sky changed and the rising sun was bright red.

Choctaw came out and we went down the steps and out to the car. Little Wind let the screen bang as she came out. She lifted her hand to Choctaw. "Don't get killed."

"Not planning on it," he said.

The world was no longer red and black now, but honey-gold. We climbed in the car and I put on my hat and drove us away, back to Hootie Hoot to find horses.

IN TOWN WE were able to find a place where I could buy a better trail hat of the sort I used to wear, though the tan one I picked out was a bit tall on my head as far as I was concerned, so I gave it a deep crease. We then went over to the livery, which is always a good place to start when you're looking for someone.

When we got there a white fellow about the height and width of an ancient tree stump, but brisk acting as a squirrel who'd been in the coffee grounds, met us with a smile that contained all his teeth, and seemed to contain someone else's too. It was the widest, whitest smile I'd ever laid eyes on, except for a picture of a shark I'd seen in a book.

"What can I do you gentlemen for?" he said. "I'm Angelo."

"Two good rent horses would be the most important, plus the tack that goes with it," I said.

"Well now," he said, "I think I can fix you gentlemen up."

There were several horses in stalls chewing on hay, and there was a small pig rooting about in the hay and horse shit on the floor of the run-through. There was a wagon, a couple of buggies, and a bicycle. Off to one side at the back of the place was an anvil and a forge and a blower, and hung on the wall were blacksmithing tools.

The horses he showed us looked to have been dug up from being dead a week and held up with a stick. One of them looked at me in a manner that said, "Shoot me, please."

"Why them ain't good horses," Choctaw said. "What you take us for?"

"Well, I got horses for white people and colored. These are for colored and Indians, which it appears to me, between the two of you, that bill is filled."

"Are the horses making the choice who rides them?" I said.

"Of course not," Angelo said.

"Then that means you're making that choice," I said. "Which also means it's you we got a bone to pick with, or maybe pick out of you."

"Well, now. I don't have to rent you no horses at all."

"Listen here, we got cash money," I said, and I did, as I had cashed in one of the vouchers back in Fort Worth, "and we want to rent horses, but not a couple that might die on us before we get out of town."

"I think those two might die straining to shit," Choctaw said.

That's when I noticed one of the other horses, a much better one, and it looked damn familiar. I went closer and looked at it in the stall. It was the white and chestnut paint my son had been riding. It had not been gelded. It looked sturdy and strong and had what I like to call a feisty eye. Not as much as my old cayuse Satan, but somewhat like it.

"I know a colored fellow rode this one," I said. "I seen him on it."

"Lots of paints," Angelo said.

"No. This is the one. I might also mention that we are the law."

"You?"

"Us." I showed him my papers.

"There are colored lawmen?"

"I rode as a Marshal for Hanging Judge Parker," I said. "Now I'm riding for the railroad. Or hope to ride, but we need a couple of horses, and I think that paint is one of them."

Angelo touched a hand to his chin. He had gone crafty thinking about that government money and how he could suck out of us more than what a couple horses were worth. I saw it coming.

"Now, knowing you two work for the law, that's different. I'm thinking that paint there, and the gear goes with it, another horse, say that black gelding there, would both go well."

"They would. You got a price in mind?" I said.

"Well, I think I do." He told us.

"Goddamn," Choctaw said, "you're really putting the Jesse James to us."

"As a reminder," Angelo said, "it's not coming out of your pocket."

"No reason to charge double," I said, "and that's double."

"You know what," Choctaw said, "we'll just drive over to the next town, as I know the livery man there, and unlike you, he ain't no crook."

"You don't know him."

"Do."

"No, you don't."

"Do too."

"Don't."

"Stop," I said. "Listen. Here's the deal. I'll pay you half of what you asked for, and add a bit for you to keep my car in your livery, not to be driven about by anyone, especially you. If them pigeons in your loft there shit on it, I want it wiped and washed clean. I think the money I'm offering is more than you would get out of my pocket, less than what you asked of the railroad, but a good deal for you nonetheless."

Angelo rubbed his chin like he was softening an apple. "Well now," he said. "I suppose that's quite all right. But for how long?"

"We go over a week, I'll pay you more for the rent of the horses. I tell you what. We'll buy the horses. I'll pay the price you asked to own them, and I'll pay you more for watching the car if it takes more than a week."

"But I still got to clean the pigeon shit after the week?"

"You do," I said.

"I get more out of renting horses in the long run, than selling them."

"I am offering you a good railroad price. I have cash money, but I also have a voucher you will have to accept, but it's good at the bank. Any bank, I measure."

"Very well, it's a deal."

"One more thing," I asked. "That paint horse, how did you come by it?"

"I'm not in the habit of telling out of school."

"Are you," Choctaw asked, "in the habit of having your ass whipped all over this stable and stuck in your fucking forge and beat with a fucking hammer? Is that a habit you would like to acquire, though you would only have that goddamn habit once?"

"Now listen here," Angelo said.

"Shut up, Angelo," Choctaw said. "You tell us now where you got that paint."

Angelo studied Choctaw whose face had gone red and he was standing on his toes as if he might leap a great distance. Maybe on Angelo's head.

"There was some local boys come in here, and a couple of colored fellows, and they wanted to sell their horses and they took in their place a wagon and two mules and a sack of oats, but kept one chestnut horse that a colored boy was riding. They loaded their saddles and saddle bags that went with the horses they sold, all their personal goods, and put them in the wagon, and rode out of here."

"Can you run a wagon up in those mountains?"

"Not far, but there's a road. You could run that car up there for a good way before you couldn't run it at all. Up in them mountains, going from here, you'd really want horses."

"Them that got the wagon. Know who they are?" I said.

"Well, sir, couple of them. The Albright boys. Rest I don't. I seen the white fellows around. The two colored boys was new to me."

"That's all?" I said.

"All I saw."

"Where do the Albrights stay?"

"Well now, that could cause me a ripple."

"I'm going to cause you a ripple," Choctaw said.

"I do not respond well to threats."

"Don't matter how you'll respond," Choctaw said, "you'll take an ass whipping and like it, and I may have you write me a little paper on the joys of it, and I'll expect accuracy, though I may have to have Nat read it out loud to me."

"Well, now, if you insist," Angelo said. He seemed to be taking it all in stride, and not as personal as I might have. I figured with him being an asshole he dealt with pushback daily and had come to consider it as part of a day's work.

"You say 'well now' one more time and I'm coming unglued, fellow," Choctaw said.

Angelo gave us some directions that included going up high into the Arbuckle Mountains, and turning where the granite rock was slightly pink near a tree that was forked and tall and wide with big limbs, and then he said go two hoots and a holler to the right of the trail, and a yelp or two, then go on cat feet into a kind of valley where the Albright cabin stands.

Angelo explained it really wasn't the Albrights who owned it, but they had some quarrel with the family that did, and the family disappeared, including the horses, mules and a yellow dog, and then the Albrights and their ruffians moved in. It saddened me to think Rufus was one of the ruffians.

"You'll know it right off," Angelo said. "It looks like God took a shit and they made a house out of it."

Not exactly spot on directions, but it sounded possible.

"The law didn't go out to see the Albrights on the house and the family murder matter?" I said.

"The law around here has better sense."

"Here's an extra note," I said. "You best not be pulling my dick on this, or I will come back and let Choctaw take to you. Directions prove good, might be more money in it for you. If you see them boys before we do, I appreciate you don't speak of us."

"What should keep me from speaking?" Angelo said.

"You did hear that part about Choctaw wanting to take you to the anvil, use the hammer on you?" I said. "We get an inkling we have been, if you will pardon the expression, railroaded, then you're going to wish a train had run over you full of cattle and bricks, rather than have us coming back with a feeling of disappointment."

"Well now...sorry. I do understand what you're saying, and we have a deal. But I'm going to need ten more Yankee dollars to keep my mouth shut."

I was exhausted. "Fair enough."

{ 9 }

WE GOT THE horses and saddles and such to go
with them, and then we loaded a reasonable
amount of goods out of the car and into saddle
bags and a tow sack that I tied on my saddle horn. It
was only partial full, as I didn't want all that I had
brought to be a burden to the horse. I left the rest in the
car, and even traded some of what we owed for a jar
of beets Angelo spied and wanted. I had the beets and
even I didn't want them.

I wrote down everything else I left, and made Angelo
sign the paper, then kept that copy to check against our
goods when we came back. I had a feeling Angelo might
be light fingered.

Choctaw carried a couple bags of oats for the horses
hanging on his saddle horn, one bag on either side, and
we rode until we come to the hoot and holler part. It

was still a few hours to dark. We stopped at the big fork tree Angelo had told us about, and made our camp.

We strung us a rope between the big tree and a smaller one, and tied off our horses to that. We removed the saddles and fed our mounts and curried them, then me and Choctaw set about making a camp.

That forked tree was a big one, and as it looked like rain, we made a bit of a tent out of our rain coats by stringing them from tree limbs, then settled down to a cold camp.

I tell you, I missed my coffee, and the canned meat I had brought was hard to open with a pocket knife. After considerable deliberation and two shallow wounds to my hand, I got it done only to be served a meat with a congealed gel of fat coating it. It tasted like it had been cut and not cured from the assholes of dozens of cows, and only the bad part of the assholes. But we ate it, and drank some water from our canteens.

"It ain't my cooking, I can tell you that for sure," Choctaw said. "I have become quite a cook. Had to. Little Wind won't cook a damn thing, but then again, she does have the money and hires the serious things done. I haven't had to mend a fence once. I feed the chickens and hogs sometimes, but mostly I sit on my ass, or go fishing or hunting, and me and her do a lot of humping."

"Good for you, Choctaw. Sounds like you're missing home."

"I am, but that don't mean I ain't glad to be here. Smell that wet air. Rain's coming. Ain't that the best smell you can imagine, besides bacon and eggs?"

"Maybe as good as bacon and eggs, except for not being able to eat it."

We hadn't been there long until we heard a clattering, and an old white man riding a bay and leading a mule loaded down with clattering pots and pans came along the trail. He had the sinking sun to his back and he was short and stocky and had his stirrups set high. His black hat looked beat down at the crown and the brim drooped like it was sad. He wore a coat too heavy for the weather. He wore a big old pistol that had once been cap and ball before being converted to cartridges. It was stuck in a holster about the size of a saddle bag hanging off his hip. He spied us, of course, and paused in front of our little camp. I could smell him from three feet away. It was an odor like woodsmoke, unbathed skin, and dried blood from skinning animals. In some way or another he looked familiar. He let his hands rest on his saddle horn.

"Howdy, boys?"

"Howdy," I said.

"You got any coffee?" the old man asked.

"Sorry. Making a cold camp."

"Say you are. Why is that?"

"We're lazy," Choctaw said, and grinned at the man on the horse who grinned back. "We can give you some cold canned meat, but you might prefer chewing on one of your boots."

"I reckon I'll pass on that one," the old man said. "What you gentlemen all about?"

"Hunting a little," I said.

"Hunting what?"

"Squirrels."

"There's plenty of them."

"Why we're hunting them, starting tomorrow. Just a stretch of time to shake the town dust off and get some mountain air."

"You wouldn't want to buy some pots and pans, would you? That's my trade, selling pots and pans."

"Got plenty of them," I said.

"Well, boys, if you ain't in the market for pots and pans, and all you got is bad meat and no coffee, I'll be passing on. Good luck on the squirrels. A mess of them cooked just right are good eating. Lot better than rat."

"A side of dandelion greens sets it off nice," Choctaw said.

The man touched his hat and rode on then. I looked at Choctaw and he looked at me. Choctaw said, "We might want to try and stay alert tonight."

"Yeah, I don't cotton much to that fellow," I said. "Even his mule looked shifty."

The air started smelling stronger, fresh and wet and pleasant, but I was less enthused with the rain when it came, as it brought not only dampness but a chill wind. Still, we had made our camp good and the tree was on a rise, and the rain was coming down pretty straight, so under the rain coat tent we stayed, if not dry, short of miserable. The horses, though, had to take it, and there was nothing else for it.

Listening to the rain I felt for a time as if I was in mine and Ruthie's old home in Fort Smith, Arkansas, and that we were lying in bed with the children little and asleep, the rain pelting the window, and there in my dream Ruthie and I were young and I was holding her and listening to her breathe in deep sleep, and then I awoke to realize it was Choctaw breathing, but at least I wasn't holding him. Our staying alert plan hadn't lasted long. We had turned into old men and had fallen asleep. Still, nobody came back and killed us, so all was good.

At first light the rain was gone. We crawled out from under our tent and by the time we had packed up and wrung out our rain coats, taken care of the horses, it was already warm. It was funny how fast the temperature could change in the mountains, and how a rain could make a summer night seem like a winter morning. Below us, we could hear last night's water draining through a granite crack in the mountains, and the sound of its gurgling was like a young girl's laughter.

We rode along in the early morning light, the sun rising up slowly, the air and earth still dark with the remains of night, measuring in our heads what we thought of as how far the sound from a man's hoot could go, as well as a couple of hollers. It's not exact mapping, but it's an old way of telling a trail.

Figuring we was through the hoot, and maybe one holler, I noticed in the distance a blink of light, and then through the trees I saw the light was shining on window glass in a cabin down below. That meant we were actually nearly two hollers in, or our man in the town below had added one holler too many.

The house was hardly a house at all. It was a mound of dried mud and thatch stuck up against the mountain side and did indeed look like a giant turd. There was a little bit of smoke coming from a chimney that was made of tight mortared rocks. No horses were in view, and I figured that they were brought in through the double wide doors that looked like they ought to fit a castle. Having them inside they couldn't be stolen, and on a cool, mountain night their body heat kept the place warm, if most likely stinky of horse shit.

Just as the sun rose higher, I saw yet another wink, but this from a tall oak that was on the edge of where the trail dipped off and the turd house was visible. Choctaw saw it too.

We both recognized it as sunlight on metal, and we got off our horses fast and led them down to the side of the trail and into a draw.

"Think he seen us?" I said.

"Way the sun is rising, he sure could have. I figure he was waiting for us to get closer. They must have known we was coming and set a watchman," Choctaw said. "I don't reckon whoever is in that tree has been there all night. Not with the weather we had. If they were there, they would have been more than a mite miserable."

"The pot and pan salesman must have told them of our approach. And now I know who he reminded me of. He looks like he might be kin to Angelo."

"That bastard turned on us. We'll have to get that ten dollars back."

"Maybe a patch of his hide to go with it."

"Reckon he warned them and this morning early they got a man to hide in that tree," Choctaw said. "Goddamn assassin."

We tied our horses off to some brush. I pulled my Winchester and scooted up the rise and took a peek. I sat still for a long time, looking through a split in the brush. He was within rifle shot for a good rifle and a good shooter. I had a rifle of my own, and I was a good shooter, but I didn't cotton right then to shooting him off a limb like a squirrel, since I didn't plan to eat him.

I heard a crack from that tree, and it was a seriously loud one, because the tree was a good way off, and then a colored man fell out of the tree like a ripe apple, riding a broken limb to the ground, which was a solid drop of about twenty feet. He had been holding a rifle, but when he smacked the ground it went sailing into the brush along with his hat. When he hit, he screamed like a panther, and I could hear him moaning and groaning all the way where I was.

"Come on up, Choctaw, and bring the horses."

I scooted toward the fallen shooter on foot, and when I got to the top of the trail, I started trotting. When I got closer, I cocked the Winchester, and then Choctaw came along riding his horse, leading mine. I climbed on my ride and we rode up on the fellow, who was lying on the ground, screeching. The tree limb had broken in such a way that a long fragment of it had been driven up between his legs, through his pants, and into his balls. He had his hand on his revolver, but he didn't have the strength or the thought to pull it.

I swung off my horse and pointed the Winchester at him. His face was covered in sweat, and blood and piss had soaked his pants, the ground, and the broken shaft of the tree. The white, split part of the broken limb had turned brown from his blood.

"That there was quite a fall," Choctaw said, always one to state the obvious.

"Oh, Jesus, Jesus," the man said. "Mother. Oh, God. Mother."

I went over and kneeled beside him and took his pistol from its scabbard and tossed it aside.

"I ain't doing so good," he said.

I leaned over and checked the shaft. "It's deep," I said.

"Don't you think I don't know that? Oh, my Lord Jesus and all his flock. Oh, Jesus it hurts. Shoot me. Just shoot me. I ain't a man no more. I can feel my dick is up in my ass, or something."

"Or something," I said.

"Can you help me?"

"I don't know," I said.

"Listen here, son," Choctaw said. "You fucked up when you rode with this bunch. That pot and pan salesman tell you we was coming?"

"Angelo sent him," the young man said. "They're cousins."

"As we figured," Choctaw said, still sitting on his horse.

"The other colored boy, Rufus, he still with you?" I said. "Listen, I know it's hard to talk, but you got a chance to redeem yourself if you're willing."

"Rufus? He don't go by Rufus, if that's him. Calls himself Jim."

"Nonetheless."

"Yes. God, Jesus, and the Holy Fucking Ghost. Just pull this stick out of me."

"Do that, you'll flood blood and won't last more than a few minutes."

"Going to die anyway."

"Probably," I said. "How are they set down there?"

"They sent me to pick you off. I can shoot better than the others, except for Jim. He's good."

"Learned from me."

"You?"

"I'm his father."

"Shit. I saw you through the train window. You're a conductor."

"Porter," I said.

"I don't know train shit," he said. "I don't hurt anymore though."

"You're draining out, son. I can promise you a burial out here. Good place to rest. It's pretty."

"My name is Gerald Cunningham. Them down there know me as Thomas. I am from Lawton here in Oklahoma. My mother's name is Maxi. Can you tell her what happened to me, but leave out the bad parts?"

"I ain't telling Maxi shit," Choctaw said. "You was going to shoot us."

"I'll get word to her," I said.

He wasn't talking after that. His eyes were hazy looking, like a blue norther had moved into them. Choctaw got off his horse and took the boy's feet, and I lifted him under the arms and we set him, stick and all, against the tree he had fallen out of. He wasn't dead, but his shadow was already crossing the River Styx, just slowly.

"We'll come back and bury him," I said.

[103]

"You can bury him. He was going to shoot us."

"Yeah. And now we're going down to shoot them. My boy maybe as well."

"We won't do that."

"Choices may be few," I said.

{ 10 }

WE RODE DOWN the rise and stayed out of rifle shot, stopped under a tree, pulled our long guns, dismounted, and stared at the big turd with thin, white smoke floating out of the chimney like it was oozing souls.

I seen then someone was moving past the window, and then one of the big doors opened, and then the other, and my son came out leading a chestnut horse and carrying a rifle.

He raised a hand at me, like we were just doing a howdy to each other, and started up the hill.

"Should I pick him off?" Choctaw said.

"That's my son."

"Then that's a no. Shit, I should have known by his ears."

I held my rifle down by my side and started walking toward him. When I was within comfortable earshot, he said, "Ain't no one in there now, Daddy."

"Rufus, you idiot."

"I know."

When he got up close to me, I looked him over. He seemed in fine enough shape, a little thin, maybe, a little older looking in the face, like he had had a vision of his future and it was on fire and smoldering. He had a pistol stuck in his belt.

"Where's the rest of your gang?"

"I done left them."

"Little late."

"I ain't killed nobody."

"You been with them that killed," I said.

"Yes, sir," he said, and he was more like my son than he had been in a few years. That defiance had left his face. He reminded me of when he was a little boy and I had caught him stealing chickens from a neighbor, made him take the chickens back, plus one of ours, and apologize.

"So, they aren't in the house down there?"

"They went out the back way. That mound house fits into a cave, and it's open in the back. I told them I was done, and I thought they was going to shoot me, but I said I'd go out and waste time and mislead you, so that let me out of there alive."

"You're misleading us then?"

"Supposed to be, but no sir. Listen, Daddy, I can tell you which way they went, and after that, I know Choctaw there can follow them."

"You don't know Choctaw."

"That's him up the hill, ain't it?"

"Yeah."

"I recognized him from your stories. You got lots of stories."

"They ain't stories, Rufus. They are events."

"Yes, sir. I didn't tell them I'm your son, but I told them who you were and told stories about you to make them fear you, but I think it just excited them. Still, they didn't want to tangle this morning. Charlie Albright ate something gave him a bellyache. He wants to get over that before he kills you. He don't want a shootout on a sick stomach."

"Where are these gangsters going so Charlie can wear off a bellyache?"

"They went out the back of the cave but didn't tell me where they're going. They left the wagon and took the mules. They left out early, but they just took the essentials, meaning the money, and left. I let them have my part. You can come down and see."

"You're my son, and I want to believe you, but boy, you have put yourself in the wrong saddle as of late."

"Yes, sir. I have made a major mistake and become a major disappointment, but there ain't a thing in the world that would have made me lead you into disaster."

"How do you know they aren't using you to set us up?"

"Because they're long gone, like I was saying. Except for Thomas. He was supposed to scout you, maybe pull an ambush. They didn't let him know they were leaving. Just decided he was expendable. I didn't argue none. They saw me as expendable too, as I hadn't been a part of their gang for long. They let me come talk to you so they could leave. They didn't tell me that, but I could figure it. They knew I wasn't ever going to ever fit in like they wanted. I'm surprised they didn't kill me. The Albright boys have whims."

"Thomas, who said his name was actually Gerald, fell out of a tree and got a stick up his balls so bad he's bleeding out. We left him lying against a tree."

"Shit," he said. "He shouldn't have gone. They sent him out hoping he might clip one or both of you. I could hardly take it, because I knew it was you coming. Day I saw you on the train, I knew then you'd be coming."

I yelled at Choctaw, "Rufus is coming up. He claims to have abandoned them."

"Come up, Rufus," Choctaw said.

"Give Choctaw your rifle," I said, "and your pistol. Tell him I'm going down."

—⁕—

I snuck along the edge of a small ridge and worked myself to the side, then inched down using brush and rocks to hide behind as best I could, expecting the possibility of a bullet.

Finally, I was at the side of the turd house, and from there I inched my way toward the door, holding my rifle at the ready.

I eased up to the doors and took a quick gander. All that was in there was the sparky remains of a fire in the fireplace and the smell of horseshit and sweaty men.

Inside, I prowled around, and went through the house and into the cave, which was good sized. That's where the horses had been kept. They had left memories of themselves in stinky piles. The wagon they had got from Angelo was inside and there were some food goods in the back of it that they'd left in their hurry to leave. Mules would be a faster way to go than a clunky wagon.

The back of the cave had a big opening and it had been covered with brush, the brush now thrown to the side of the gap. So far, everything Rufus had told me checked out.

Walking out, I went around a curve of a trail, going Indian quiet. I saw their sign and it led around another curve and behind a hill. I couldn't know for sure, but I had a feeling they weren't back there waiting on me, but had gone on to let Charlie nurse his stomach ache. Still, I decided not prowl around that next curve by myself.

I walked out and back up the hill to Choctaw and Rufus.

"Gone, huh?" Choctaw said.

"Yep."

"Rufus here was just telling me about Charlie Albright and his bellyache."

I told Choctaw about the gap at the back through the cave, the trail I had followed briefly.

"I'll scout it. You two stay here. You hear gunfire, come running. I'll leave my horse and go on foot."

Choctaw took his rifle and started easing down the hill toward the turd house. We were silent as we watched him go, reach the opening of the house, and going through. He still moved smooth and swiftly.

We tied up the horses to some brush, sat down on the ground beneath a tree.

"I'm sorry, Daddy."

"Sorry don't always get it, son."

"I know. I'll take my medicine."

"You'll have to. Might have to serve some time."

"I know. I didn't understand what I was and who I was until I was with them."

"Being like them, you mean."

"No. Being unlike them. I just wanted to have adventure, like you."

"Days were different then. Even the sun seemed to crawl slower across the sky. But I didn't never rob nobody of nothing, Rufus. I was on the right side of the law, though I had occasion to protect myself from folks on both sides of the fence. But I wasn't ever no outlaw."

"I don't know what I was thinking."

"You weren't thinking. I'm glad your mother isn't around to see this."

"So am I. Listen, Daddy, you do what you have to do with me, but not before I help you stop them boys. I owe a debt to that man was shot on the train."

"Ain't no way to pay that debt in full," I said.

"I can pay as much of it as I can pay. Just let me stay with you until you've caught them."

"Or killed them."

"That too."

I thought about it. "Until then."

I T WAS LATE afternoon when Choctaw came back, walking swiftly up the hill.

"They've hightailed all right. I followed the trail a good piece, and they're making a horseshoe back toward town. I think they might actually have been scared of us, Nat. Or, Charlie had a really serious tummy ache."

"It was bad," Rufus said. "I think he nearly shit out his brains."

"Might be heading to a doctor, which is why they horseshoed," I said. "Most likely just some place to hole up until it passes."

"Makes sense But whatever their reason, they've given it up and gone back."

"They have people that support them in town," Rufus said.

"And one of those supporters would be Angelo the blacksmith and livery bastard and cousin to pot and pan man," Choctaw said.

This wasn't a question from Choctaw, and like him, I was seriously angry at that fellow. Angelo had sent the pot and pan man to see our spot. He didn't do anything himself, as he saw we were at the ready, but he warned the Turd in the Wall Gang, who sent one man to ambush us, and he was stupid enough to go, not expecting them to abandon him over a bellyache.

"Charlie hadn't been sick, they might have fought it out," Rufus said. "I built you two up big, though, so maybe that had something to do with it."

"I'm sure there wasn't any exaggeration," Choctaw said, "as we are indeed dangerous folk."

"Indeed," I said.

Rufus said, "I've made a mess of things."

"You have," I said.

"You made a bad choice, boy," Choctaw said. "I've made a few. But you're no murderer, and you've made the right choice now."

"Don't make him feel good," I said.

"Telling it true. Everything isn't black and white, Nat. Hell, this boy was sowing wild oats and he didn't sow them in blood."

"There's a dead man that would disagree with that," I said. "Rufus may not have killed him, but he was with them that did."

"He didn't know that was going to happen."

"I didn't," Rufus said, "but I knew their reputation. Thanks for the kind words, Choctaw, but I knew better and didn't act better."

"Let me ask an important question," I said. "Do those boys have fast shooting weapons?"

"They both have auto-pistols, and a Browning automatic rifle they keep hidden out at the blacksmith's shop."

"That bastard," Choctaw said.

"It's on account of the boys fight over it when they are on the road with it, so they keep it there when they're doing a small job. They're saving it for when they go into bank robbing in bigger towns. So far it's just been small banks, but they got bigger banks in mind."

"Which towns?" Choctaw said.

"Any with a good size bank. Their idea is, they go in, and if there's the slightest resistance, they open up with that Browning. They want the chance to kill people. Once I realized that, Daddy, I wanted out. I really did. But I had to go at it slowly. I was in on the train robbery, but I didn't want to be. I know how that sounds, but I didn't."

"So, while we're here talking," I said, "they're going to get that big gun? That's what they're doing, bellyache or no bellyache. I had someone after me, I'd arm myself with the heavy stuff."

"They would figure themselves safe in Hootie Hoot. It's not that all the people there love them, but most are afraid of them, and they got supporters on account of they hand money out to the right folks."

"Like Angelo and the pots and pans man," I said.

"And the sheriff."

"We'll track them and go that way," Choctaw said, "but it makes sense they'll go back to town for the gun, and on account of they have allies of a sort."

We packed up and headed out, passed by the ball-poked fellow under the tree. Me and Rufus got off our horses, and I pulled a camp shovel off my horse, and was going to bury him, when he moaned.

"He's alive," I said.

"Leave him," Choctaw said, still mounted. "Time will finish him."

"I can't do that," I said.

"He wasn't so bad," Rufus said, getting off his horse.

"Bad enough he was going to shoot us from a tree," Choctaw said.

"I knew you and Daddy would see him. I know your skills."

"Them skills got a coat of rust on them, right now," Choctaw said. "We were lucky that limb broke and went into his balls."

I went over and looked at him closer. He had bled out a lot. The ground was soaked. His dark skin had turned the color of ash. Flies buzzed around him like church folk at a picnic. Somehow, he was still alive.

"We got to go get the wagon, hitch the horses to it, and haul him out."

Still sitting on his horse, Choctaw said, "Or we could wait for it to be finished. He won't make sundown."

"He's lasted longer than I thought," I said, peeling back one of Gerald's eyelids. The eyes seemed small. The whites were pink. "Wagon will slow us, but waiting will slow us more. At least we'll be moving toward town."

"Waste of time either way," Choctaw said. "But if we're going to do it, let's do it. You stay here, Nat. Me and Rufus will hitch our horses to the wagon. Let's hope they've been trained to pull such, or we got a whole new sack of worms to open up and fish with."

"Considering they're from the livery, and Angelo looks to work all purpose, they most likely will."

"We see Angelo," Choctaw said, "I might just hitch him up to a wagon and make him pull me home. Then he can take you down to Texas."

{ 12 }

I T WASN'T A pleasant ride back to Hootie Hoot, on account of Gerald did a lot of moaning, and the sound of it made me sick. There wasn't a thing for it, though. Pulling that stick out of him would have finished him right off, and it was going to finish him anyway. Fact that he was still alive was amazing to me. He actually seemed to have become more alert, opening his eyes now and then and asking for his mama.

We had used some bedding from the turd house to wrap him up, and the way the covers lay over him and that stick poked out, it looked as if he had the biggest hard-on in all of human kind, and maybe some donkeys.

The wagon bounced over the trail as we went, and a few times he screamed out. It was as uncomfortable a trip as you can imagine, but the horses fitted up to the wagon fine. We tied off Rufus's horse to the back of the wagon.

When we were about a mile outside of Hootie Hoot, finally on level ground, Gerald got quiet and we fixed him for dead, but no sooner did we check on him than he began to moan. I checked under the covers, and he was no longer bleeding out in a big way, just little droplets. This figured, because he couldn't have much blood left in him.

We pulled up just outside of town, off the trail, not too far from where we could see the livery. We put the wagon and horses down in a damp draw behind some trees. We hustled up to the lip of the draw and looked through some bushes. It was late in the day, but still some time before dark, so we scouted and thought about things and decided if they wanted that gun that was supposedly kept at the livery, they had it by now. That gun was damn sure something to keep in mind.

"Think they might have moved on to do the bank robbery?" I said to Rufus.

"I think Charlie will want to get over his stomach ache and spend some time with his girl. She works at the saloon. The boys aren't planners in a big way. They don't take chances so much as they don't understand what a chance is. They know you'll most likely come after them, but they feel safe here in Hootie Hoot."

"Don't tell me his girl is a dance hall floozy," I said.

"She's a bartender."

"All right," I said. "We wait until dark, then sneak in on foot. You know where he holes up with this girl?"

Rufus nodded. "I do. But there's the rest of the boys, and that pot and pan salesman. My guess, except for Charlie's brother, Lowe, they'll go to the saloon. Like I said, they don't make a whole lot of plans. I think they figure they got that gun, they're in good shape. Had they had it, and had Charlie not been sick, they would have shot it out with you back up in the hills."

"What about the sheriff?"

"He gets a cut of what they rob, so he'll not be of any service to you. He won't right out and out help them, though. He'll just hole up and stay out of it."

"That's helpful information."

"I want it to be. I should never have been roped in by their bullshit, but I was, and I offer no excuses."

"Best not to, as none are accepted."

IT was bright that night, which is never good for sneaking. We had our eyes on the livery, which would be our first stop for a variety of reasons, and so far, none of us had seen Angelo leave, and there was light pouring out of the big back opening. I could hear some hammer work coming from within the place, and I figured he was working a horseshoe or some such in the forge and then on the anvil.

We unhitched the horses from the wagon and curried them and fed them, and then we saddled them in case they might be needed for a quick exit, but it was decided that I would go down by myself first, though truth was Choctaw was a better sneaker. I thought I should go because Choctaw was in a mood over Angelo, and I'd rather have not been party to him pulling out Angelo's tongue with blacksmith tongs and cutting it off with a dull knife.

Choctaw had lost some patience since I first knew him, and truth to tell, Angelo had riled me up considerable as well.

Rufus was told to remain with the horses if Choctaw were to leave. I was going to creep down there on Angelo, find out about the gun, and where all the boys might be, make sure he hadn't let pigeons shit on my car. Fifteen or so minutes later as judged by the watch in Choctaw's head, he was to come after me.

I was wearing my two pistols, my derringer, and I decided on my shotgun with the tote strap on it, and left the Winchester. Rufus had been given his pistol and Winchester back, so he was ready to back our play, whatever it might be.

—⁓—

THE crickets started up as I worked my way down. Someone with experience and a good ear can often figure when they rile like that, that something is moving nearby, but I tried to tell myself that Angelo was a town boy and might not know that, or notice on account of all that hammering, which by this time had become a consistent pinging.

I stopped briefly behind a clump of bushes, looked back at the trees where Rufus and Choctaw waited. I looked up at the moon. It was so bright you could damn near thread a needle by the light.

In the old days I wouldn't have been too worried if it was one guy, but I won't pull your big toe and tell you I was feeling fearless, because I wasn't. I hadn't never felt fearless, but I had always felt competent. But for the last few years I had ridden Pullman cars and been a servant, and that changes a fellow's nature some. I had to put my war face on and go down there and get it done.

I started moving again.

{ 13 }

CARRYING THAT SHOTGUN, I felt pretty ready, but I also knew you could pull off one easy and quick round when maybe you didn't need to. I tried to keep my nervous fingers in mind as I crept up to the livery's back doors, which were thrown wide open. I could hear that pinging sound inside, abrasive to the ear and the mind, and I was reconsidering pulling that shotgun trigger just to end that damn sound.

When I got up to the door, I peeked around, trying to be careful, and standing at the anvil, hammer raised for a strike, the other hand holding metal tongs that were gripping a horseshoe, was Angelo. And he was looking right at me.

No doubt he knew he had screwed the duck by telling his cousin to warn the Radiant Apple gang, because his face melted like candle wax, and he threw that hammer at me. I ducked back behind the edge of the livery just as the hammer knocked wood out of the door frame and sent splinters into the night followed by the hammer.

I charged in then, and by that time he was wrestling a pistol out of holster hung over an empty horse stall with a chicken roosting on it.

I ran quick, and when he pulled the pistol, I was on him. I hit him with the stock of the shotgun and knocked him flat on the ground. He lost hold of the pistol. I leaned in and picked it up and tossed it over the stall onto some nasty looking hay, startling the chicken into a cackle fest and a fluttering of wings. It sailed past me and landed on the ground clucking and running and disappeared around a stack of hay and my parked car and went quiet.

"Hello there, Angelo," I said.

"You ain't got no right to hit me like that."

He was holding his hand to his head, which was bleeding slightly and was already starting to bruise and lump up.

"I really enjoyed it, though, and frankly, I do have the right. I have the might of the railroad behind me, and if you move, I will hit you again, or I may just shoot you, and this shotgun will do more than give you a flesh wound, unless you count flesh splashed all over this livery."

"Be gentle with that thing," he said.

"You told your cousin to tell the gang where we were. That's not nice, Angelo."

"They would have hurt me."

"They didn't know you knew we were here, but you managed to tell your pot and pan kin we were, and my guess is you was planning on making not only our money, but some for them, and then afterwards, us dead, you could sell my car or ride around in it like a big dog. Also, there's pigeon shit on the windshield, so you haven't been keeping up with our bargain."

"That's chicken shit."

"I beg your pardon then."

About then Choctaw and Rufus came in carrying Gerald on a blanket they had stretched him on. They had covered him with another, so that he made a kind of sandwich. His head showed at one end, his boots at the other. The stick in his balls was poking up the blanket.

They laid Gerald down on the ground near the hay pile the chicken had gone around, not far from my car.

Angelo sat up cautiously. He looked at Gerald, then at Rufus. "You two was with the boys."

Choctaw said, "Rufus here was what they call an infiltrator. He was working for us."

"A spy?" Angelo said.

"Spy is good," Choctaw said.

"Sonofabitch," Angelo said. "What about the other fellow there...Jesus, is that his dick?"

[127]

"Even a bull elephant doesn't tote a poker like that," Choctaw said. "That there is a broken limb in his balls."

"A broken limb?" Angelo said.

"Forget it," I said. "Listen here, where's that fast-firing rifle those boys keep here?"

"They done got it. They told me y'all was dead."

"Gerald there turned out to be a poor assassin," I said. And I thought to myself, they might actually think we were dead, and that worked to our advantage.

"Fell out of a fucking tree," Choctaw said. "And Angelo, you better not be lying to me about that gun. I find it in this livery, I'll pull that stick out of Gerald and ram it in you."

"Charlie come and got it. Said he had plans for it."

"How much ammunition he got for it?" Choctaw said. "Be talky with explanation."

"Not so much. I mean, some, but not a lot. Gun is stolen and so is the ammunition. After going on a cow-killing spree, Charlie is careful with the loads. He don't know how to repack the shells, so once it's empty, he'll have some trouble finding ammo for that thing around here. He got it from some military place in Lawton, I think. It was a five-finger donation."

"All right, you roll over on your belly," I said to Angelo, and he did. "Rufus, you tie him up and pull him over behind the hay stack. Might be a chicken there, so don't scare it."

While Rufus went about that, I pulled Choctaw aside. "They're such deadly killers, why didn't they just wait here for us at the livery?"

"No one said they were smart," Choctaw said. "They may actually think we are dead, that Gerald got us. My figure is Charlie didn't have so much a stomach ache as he had a dick ache and wanted to see his gal, and the others may have their own women, or just want a drink."

We went over to where Rufus had tied up Angelo. Angelo was sitting on the ground. I couldn't tell if he was perturbed or just surprised by the whole thing.

I said, "All right, who all is on their side, and you better count right."

"The two brothers, of course. They got a man with them called the Kansas Kid. I think he gave himself that name. And there's my cousin. There's a couple of others in town. Young guns who don't know the shoot-em-up days are over. They're trying to make a name for themselves. But that don't mean they'll back the boys. They might, might not."

I looked at Rufus. "You know them?"

"I know of them, but like he says, they aren't dedicated."

"Who else?"

"That's all I know for sure," Angelo said. "Others in town might throw in with them, but mostly I think they'll just stay out of it. Sheriff's easy on them, but I doubt he'll come to their rescue. There was a big tadoo a week or so ago, some drunk Texans got into it in the saloon, and the sheriff, Titus, he locked his office door and stayed inside where it was safe. He mostly just collects taxes and insults."

"You better be telling us the truth, because you know of others, and you don't tell us, and we survive, which we plan to, we'll use you for pistol practice. First the barrels upside your head, then the bullets."

"I ain't got no cause to lie," Angelo said.

"Yeah," Choctaw said, "but you do it anyway."

ANGELO GAVE US some rundown on where the boys
might be, and Rufus, who had experience with
them, backed up his information.

Charlie Albright's girl had a room above the feed
store on Main Street, and that's where he would be
holed up, or so Rufus and Angelo thought. As for the
brother, it could be he was there too. Angelo told us the
Albright boys sometimes had fun with the same girl. I
suppose you might say it wasn't exactly true love.

As for the others, well, they liked the saloon.

Those boys weren't as smart as other bandits me and
Choctaw had dealt with, but me and Choctaw weren't
as young as we once were either. That maybe balanced
things out.

From the front door of the livery, you could look out
on Main Street, and see the window that was the girl's

room above the feed store. There wasn't any light on in the window, but then again, if Charlie, and possibly his brother, were up to what I thought they were up to, there wouldn't be.

The night was young, so the street was busy. There were electric lights on along the walkways, and coming out of a few store fronts, and the saloon. Music was coming out of there as well. A bunch of tin-eared musicians with horns and a piano that had last been tuned when it was made was clinking what might almost be called a tune. Out front of the saloon an old man sat in a rocking chair with a yellow dog under it.

A few folks were riding horses down the street. There was a fat man wobbling on a bicycle, and there were a few motor cars as well, the people in them dressed up like they were going somewhere important. Which they weren't. Not in this town.

"What I think we do," I said to Rufus, "is we go around behind the building and see about a way in there. The door by the front of the feed store might seem too obvious. That I assume has a stairway up?"

"It does. I've never been upstairs, but I've seen the door open and there's a stairway. Might be one around back."

"We'll start there. You'll go first, and I'll go through the alleyway there, and meet up with you. Don't get in a hurry. Choctaw?"

"Yep."

"You might want to gag our friend there, then scope out the saloon. They don't know you, but you can maybe peek in. They aren't going to let a half-breed in, especially since one half is colored."

"I don't know what all I am, but you're right. I'll give it a peek-a-boo and watch for anything that looks wrong. I may invite myself in, I need to. Can I shoot people?"

"A man that wouldn't kill a bobcat is now ready to shoot folks up?"

"I like bobcats better."

"Good enough. Just make sure you aren't mowing down citizens."

"I don't really like them much either, but all right."

Rufus still had the Winchester, so I sent him soft-footing out the back door and to the left. The idea was for him to edge out of town, then trot back and go behind the line of buildings on Main Street, get to the back of the feed store, see if there was a way in, and wait for me.

My plan was to stroll across the street with the shotgun held down to my side, go through an alleyway between the door that led upstairs, and the sheriff's office. There was no light in the sheriff's office. Maybe he was sleeping. Maybe he was home.

While I worked myself up to take my walk, Choctaw was lowering his pants, so as to remove his underwear

to use as a gag for Angelo's lying mouth. Once Choctaw had his pants back on, he was to go out the back door and ease around to the saloon, see if he could see inside. He didn't know who he was looking for, but I thought he'd figure a way to know who was who. Although I had a figure where at least one of the brothers might be, I might be wrong. They could be in the saloon. Shit, one of them might be the tuba player for all I knew. If they were, Choctaw had seen a wanted poster with a drawing of the brothers, so that helped. I had seen them in person, of course, as well as the one living member of the gang, and me and Choctaw had seen the pot and pan man. But there might be a couple others that had thrown in with them. That was the wild card. But Choctaw was resourceful, and I reckoned he'd make out all right when it came to figuring who was who.

"Ah, come on there, fellow, not your underwear," Angelo said as I stepped out into the street.

—◊◊—

BEING a bright night and all, I felt like a live catfish at a fish fry trying to pretend he was a wagon wheel. Anyone and everyone could see me, but even if they could, I didn't notice anyone really looking.

The street and walkways under the overhangs had gone mostly empty all of a sudden, and I could see the cars that had been in the street were parked in front of a building on down a way, and there were people going into it and light from a window and the open door was spilling out into the street. I couldn't figure what was going on there, but I was glad that's where the activity was mostly ending up, though the saloon was still doing right smart business as well. The tinkling piano and those awful horns had gotten louder, if not more melodious. Someone was hitting on a triangle, and the pinging of it damn near jerked a knot in my dick. I suspected the band had gotten louder due to the saloon crowd noise having grown rowdier.

I continued to traipse my way across the street brisk like, and nobody shot at me. I got to the alley near the door to the stairway. I tried the door for good luck, but it was locked. I slipped on down the alley and around back, as per our plan. I got to the rear of the building, and leaned my back against the wall.

There was a lonesome tree about thirty feet from me, and a hoot owl was making noise in it. I could see its eyes. Owls are interesting birds, but they always made me a smidgeon nervous, way they turned their heads and made that ghostly noise.

In short time I saw a figure coming out of the shadows, rising up out of a gulley, and I could tell by his shape it was Rufus. He trotted over to me, and we went to the back door to try it. It was also locked. We were about to see if we could pry it open with my Bowie knife, when I looked up and seen the overhang on the roof wasn't all that high up.

I had Rufus make a step for me by linking his hands, and with my shotgun strapped across my back, I put a boot in it and he boosted me up. Then I leaned down, stretching out my hand to him. He handed me the Winchester, which I laid on the roof. Then he jumped and got hold of my extended hand. His weight damn near yanked me off the roof. I clung to him, though, and locked a boot in a tin rain gutter, and pulled him up.

We stood up and eased along the overhang, me going one way, and Rufus the other, working our way around to the front of the building. The overhang creaked a little.

When I got to the end of the side overhang, close to the front, there was a gap where a water drain pipe ran up it. The gap between the water pipe and the front overhang was about two feet.

I precariously eased myself around the drain pipe, stepped wide and onto the overhang that ran in front of the window where it was thought Charlie Albright and maybe his brother were holed up. No pun intended.

I patted the papers I had for him inside my shirt as reassurance, eased toward the window as I saw Rufus coming from the other side. We ended up squatting on the overhang on opposite sides of the window.

I could hear bed springs squeaking in there, like rats at a cheese party, and I took a chance and peeked around the window frame. It was dark, but enough light was coming from the street lamps I could see inside. A man's bare ass was visible riding up and down on a spread-legged woman underneath him. Another man was sitting in a chair watching them, smoking a cigar. I could tell that the man in the chair was Lowe Albright, and it figured that the naked ass belonged to his brother, and the woman underneath him was his one true love of the moment.

I pulled back and studied on things for a moment. There was the problem of the woman, since she was an innocent bystander, though I use the word innocent freely.

Rufus took a peek, looked at me and shrugged his shoulders. I was coming up with a game plan, but I decided I needed another look to make sure things were the same as before, so that I knew where everyone was placed. I thought I might bust the window out with the shotgun barrel and take them by surprise, yell out that we were lawmen, which was kind of true.

I edged my eye to a glass pane, and there standing at the window, butt-naked, was Charlie, who a moment ago had been briskly occupied. His manly business was hanging out like a dripping turkey neck. Under his arm, I could see Lowe had started to undo his belt, and the woman was holding her arms up to him in invitation.

I looked up from the turkey neck, seen then that Charlie was looking right at me. His cheeks there in the light from the street were heated up red as the apples that gave the gang its name, and his mouth was hanging open like an armadillo burrow.

"Shit," I said.

Charlie reached out of sight and came back holding a big ass rifle with a strap on it. He stepped back in front of the window as I jerked out of sight. No sooner was my head moved to the side than there was a fast burp of gunfire and the window glass shattered, and the edge of the window frame burst into pieces.

It was that automatic rifle I had heard about.

Inside, the woman started screaming.

Well now, our plan, such as it was, had done gone to drizzly shit. Me and Rufus ran off in opposite directions along the overhang, and then there was more busting of glass, this time with the barrel of the gun. By the time Charlie was leaning out of the window I was stepping back around the drain pipe. I hadn't even tried to fire back on account of how fast those bullets were flying.

I started shinnying down the drain pipe fast as a squirrel, the strapped shotgun banging me in the back. All this time, the girl in the room was screaming something terrible.

Bullets from the roaring gun were scraping brick all around the edge of the building, and one hit the alley wall across the way, ricocheted back, and smacked above my head, showering me in brick dust.

I dropped to the ground as the bullets began to tear in a different direction. From the mouth of the alley I could see Rufus had leaped off the roof and was hauling ass toward the livery. Bullets tore into the livery wall, kicked up dirt in the street, and clipped a kid's head off as he walked along the boardwalk in front of the livery rolling a metal hoop.

There was a pause, and I used this as my moment to step out in the street and get a shot up to the window. But when I stepped out, there was Charlie standing on the overhang, wearing nothing except for a canvas belt with metal magazines poking out of pouches on it. He had a leather sling on the rifle, and it was hanging on his shoulder and he had the rifle against his hip and was pointing it toward me, his wing-wang waving howdy.

I was just able to step back under the overhang as he fired. Dirt threw up in the street and poked through the roof like it was made of glass, slamming into the board-walk, cutting through the brim of my hat and scraping down along the side of my left boot.

Pushing up against the wall, I was relieved to find that all my parts were in place, but my knees trembled and I could hear my heart pounding, and blood was throbbing in my temples.

Charlie had gone loco, was firing across the street, clipping horses, two dance hall girls who had poked their heads out of the saloon, the old fart in a rocking chair out front of it, as well as the yellow dog under the rocking chair.

I heard the magazine fall out of the rifle and heard him push another one in. I crept along under the boardwalk with the moonlight poking through the holes the rifle had made, and moved along to the end of the concealed walkway, figuring my next move.

That damn woman in the room was still screaming.

I heard Charlie yell, "Shut up!" and then I heard a short burst from the gun, and there was no more screaming. True love can be a trail cut short.

Charlie, having gotten started with the gun, began to now fire indiscriminately. He wasn't a good shot, but the gun had a lot of quick-fire power and impact. It was at this point that I learned what had been going on in that building down the way where I had seen a crowd gathering.

A wedding.

Folks came out of there and onto the boardwalk and into the street. I saw the windows in the building exploding, hats and the tops of two men's heads danced off and away, and what I figured was a bridesmaid got a bloody hole punched through her chest. A little girl carrying flowers got a leg shot out from under her and lay on the boardwalk amidst a spray of blooms, screaming as a car tire hissed air from a bullet hole.

Those that had not been hit by the barrage, leapt back into the building like frogs into a pond. An arm reached out and grabbed the wounded, screaming child and yanked her inside.

I looked along the street and saw one of about five shot down horses kicking its last spasms, and then there was a pause in the firing.

Taking that for my moment, I stepped out with my shotgun, knowing I was a little out of range, and starting to run down the street, back toward Charlie and his bullet spreader.

I was about halfway there when he managed to punch in another magazine, and was about to cut down on me, when the magazine jammed and he said "Shit" and a bullet said splat, and took the side of Charlie's face off. Charlie did a kind of sideways hop to the edge of the overhang, and fell off in the street on his back. Some piece from his face, a jawbone, I guess, was swirling around in the street like a roulette wheel.

Rapid Winchester fire started blasting from the window, toward where Charlie's killing shot had come from, which was the livery. I saw Rufus duck inside with his rifle, as Lowe's Winchester splattered lead against the wood slats and punched through them like fingers through fog.

I had gotten closer now, and standing in the street, near the boardwalk, I cut down with the shotgun on the

window and the rifle poking out of it. There was a loud grunt, and the Winchester poked back inside. About that time there came firing from the saloon. Shotguns and pistols and a last moment hooting from horns and a loud pound on the piano.

Appeared Choctaw had run into a spot of trouble.

{ 15 }

AS I WAS running across the street toward the saloon, Lowe came out through the alley, having climbed down the back stars and come around to the street. He looked wild. He made a quick glance at his brother, lying in the street with the moon shining on his naked butt, and then came at me, stepping into the street firing his Winchester.

One of his shots hit my shotgun and made it ping and fly away from my throbbing hands.

As Lowe was cocking his Winchester, I drew my Peacemaker in the manner I had learned, which was what some called "Go fast slowly."

I raised the pistol calm as a fat preacher with all the offering money and a fast horse, just as another Winchester shot lifted my hat and creased my hair. My vision had narrowed into a long, tight tunnel, and as

Lowe, angry and impetuous, was walking toward me cocking the Winchester, I fired.

Lowe yelled and his legs went out from under him. I had hit him in the belly and it had knocked him down like his pockets were filled with weights. The Winchester flew from his hands and skidded onto the dirty street.

Somewhere a man yelled from concealment, "That'll teach him."

While Lowe groaned in pain, he scrambled to pull what I saw was an automatic pistol, but before I could put him on his path to absolute darkness, a shot accommodated him, caught him in the side of the head and he fell over.

It was Rufus. He had stepped out of the livery and popped him with his Winchester. He had killed both of the brothers. Their cheeks would shine no more.

Now Rufus threw the Winchester aside, it being empty I presumed, and walked over and picked up Charlie's rifle and Lowe's automatic pistol.

"Choctaw needs us," I said.

We ran to the saloon and stood on either side of the doorway, which was wide open.

I took a peek around the edge and seen what kind of business was going on.

One of the members of the band was lying on the floor clutching a tuba. He was still alive. I could see his eyes fluttering, but he was being as still as possible. There was a thin trickle of blood coming from him, making a little dark creek across the floor, dripping between a gap in the planks. Other band members were crouching down, clutching trombones and trumpets and one had that damnable triangle. Saloon patrons had hit the floor, or ducked behind tables and chairs.

I scanned the room, saw that Choctaw had shot the fellow I had seen on a horse that day with the gang. One Angelo said called himself the Kansas Kid. He was dead and leaning over the back of the piano. His hand dangled toward the piano keys and his pistol swung from his trigger finger. There were blood drops on the keys.

Pushed up tight against the wall was the pot and pan man. He had a pistol in one hand and a dance hall gal in the other, having pulled her in front of him. "Cowards," he yelled. "All three of you are on me."

That's when I finally saw where Choctaw was. He had ducked down behind the bar, and sitting in a chair behind the bar was what I figured was the bartender. He was dead with a hole through his head and his head was thrown back and his neck rested on the back of the chair and held him in place. The mirror behind him had a hole in it and there were cracks running out from the hole in all directions, one of which went all the way to the top where a small triangle of glass had come loose of it.

Choctaw was leaning over the bar. He had his shotgun lying on the bar top, and in his hand was a pistol.

"Choctaw," I said. "Me and Rufus are out here."

"Well," Choctaw said, "come on in if you like, but mind the gunfire that might kick up."

Pot and Pan Man said it again. "All three of you are on me. It ain't fair."

"We don't play fair," I said.

Pot and Pan Man glanced toward the doorway.

"Me neither," he said. "Come in here, I'll put a hole in her head big enough for a horse to fuck."

"That's not very nice," I said.

Rufus whispered across the doorway to me. "Should I go around back?"

"Yeah," I said.

As soon as I saw Rufus reach the end of the board-walk and duck into the alley to head toward the rear, I stepped into the saloon.

"Well now, showing yourself, that's not smart," Pot and Pan Man said.

I walked with my pistol down by my side. I got so I was facing him and the saloon girl. "How's this going to end, fellow?"

"Now, that there is a good question, my dusky friend. I'm thinking it ends with me waltzing out of here with this little darling, that I'll take with me to keep for a cold night. Otherwise, I get any grief from you or him behind the bar, anyone else you got with you, I'll shoot her."

"And what if I don't care if you shoot her?"

"That does produce a problem. I'm going to guess you really do care."

All I could see of him was the side of his face, one eye, and the gun pressed against the side of the girl's head.

"I will shoot you," I said.

"Nobody is that good a shot."

"He is," Choctaw said.

"I doubt that," Pot and Pan Man said.

He had no more spoken when I brought my gun up and fired. The shot whistled by the saloon girl's head so close she gasped. Pot and Pan Man gasped too. Where his right eye had been exposed there was now a bloody hole.

He slid down the wall with a bloody smear behind him, the gore coming from the exit wound in the back of his head.

The saloon girl leapt away like a deer, darted out the door and onto the boardwalk. I could hear her feet running along the boards.

"You don't miss much, do you?"

"Not much."

Rufus entered through the back way with the machine pistol in his hand.

"I see you done wrapped up the meat in butcher paper," Rufus said.

"Reckon so," I said.

"Hey," said the trombone player, standing up. "No colored allowed in here."

"Oh, shut up," Rufus said.

—⚟—

THERE wasn't any of the gang's friends that wanted any part of what had happened. I don't know if they actually had any friends in there. The two fellows Angelo mentioned either weren't there or stayed quiet.

Choctaw was pouring himself a stiff drink and had pulled a bottle of sarsaparilla out from under the counter for me.

"Everyone, drinks are on the house," Choctaw said, and became the bartender as men and saloon girls rushed the bar.

Rufus said to Choctaw, "I'll have a whisky."

"No, you won't," Choctaw said. "You'll have a sarsaparilla like your old man. And you'll like it."

"Yes, sir," Rufus said.

{ 16 }

WE STAYED IN the saloon until a lot of the whisky was drank up by the crowd, and me and Rufus had cleaned out the sarsaparilla.

Bloated on the sweet stuff, I went out back and took a piss in a ditch. I felt right then like I could fill it.

I had just buttoned up, when I heard something behind me. I wheeled. Both my pistols seemed to have hopped into my hands.

"Easy," said a man. He was short and stout and had a short-brimmed hat and eyebrows thick enough to teach circus tricks. He looked nervous as a mail order bride. He wore a sheriff's star.

"Where you been?" I said.

"I guess I was sleeping sound."

"That seems unlikely."

"Don't get smart with me, boy."

"My credentials trump yours. I work for the railroad, so don't call me boy, and don't get smart with me."

This business, a colored man talking to him like that, didn't set right with him, but he was too big a coward to make anything of it, and I hadn't lowered my pistols yet.

He smiled at me.

"There's a lot of dead folks and horses and a kid in the street, bodies in the saloon."

"They started it. And I think you'll find a yellow dog out there too. Folks responsible for all the shooting were the Albrights. Them they call the Radiant Apple gang. My understanding is with them dead, you'll be losing some income."

"What's that supposed to mean?"

"You know what it means."

The sheriff cleared his throat. "I done called out the undertaker. Let's go to the office and talk."

"Let's go to the livery first. Got a gang sympathizer there who set a man on us, and there's what I figure to be a dead man lying under a blanket." I gave the sheriff a brief explanation of why there was a colored man with a stick in his balls lying in the livery. I also mentioned we might want to check on the girl bartender in Charlie and Lowe's room.

—◊◊◊—

GERALD was still alive, believe it or not. He hadn't improved, though. He still had one foot in the outhouse hole and was hanging by a cobweb.

The surprise was Angelo had choked on Choctaw's underwear, which had a wide shit stain in the seat. I saw that when the sheriff pulled it out of his mouth. I needed to talk to Choctaw about washing his shorts more frequently, but on the other hand, it wasn't a subject I wanted to bring up. Maybe he just needed to wipe his ass better.

"Guess him strangling like that is on us," I said.

I won't lie to you. I didn't feel that bad about it. That sonofabitch tried to get us killed.

The sheriff tried to make a thing of it, but I wouldn't have a bit of it. I touted my credentials again and said as how we had gotten rid of a notorious gang, and the bodies we had stacked up like cordwood had bounties on them. I noted too that me and my crew, and I included Rufus in this, would be paid a set amount by the railroad, and the sheriff, as town lawman, might have a reward coming.

Now this perked the sheriff up. He was already counting his money, but I knew the railroad wouldn't pay him so much as a goat fart, not after I told them how he didn't do so much as even yell encouragement to us. I also planned to mention it was said he had been taking a payment from the gang all along. I couldn't prove that part, but it would go into my report.

Morning came, and all the outlaw bodies were stacked up along the outside saloon's wall. They had wrapped a blanket around Charlie's pecker, and put a patch over his face where his jaw was shot up. Neither of the brothers had red cheeks now; they had turned white as snow patches.

All of the desperadoes, as the town was now calling them, had their picture taken by a photographer, and some folks paid to have their picture taken with them. Even Gerald, who had finally died and had the stick pulled out of his balls, was propped up. They wrapped a shirt around his bloody pants. The stick was not given a position on the wall. The photographer said he could have some postcards made up of them if I wanted one. I didn't.

I heard the little girl had only taken a bad shot in the leg, and that she would recover. If the gang had any supporters in town, they didn't show that support. I think with Charlie opening up on men and women, children, horses and a dog, it had soured them on the Albrights and their disciples.

Later, when me and the sheriff went upstairs to where Charlie and Lowe had been with the female bartender, they found her naked on the bed with her side all shot up from where Charlie had opened up on her in his need to end her screaming. It was a sad case, but damn, that girl could scream.

The sheriff said, "There's two bartenders dead now. I guess the saloon will be hiring."

He looked at me like I might want to consider the job. I did not.

{ 17 }

NEXT MORNING, I bought a new hat by walking like a white man into a general store and picking one out. No one gave me trouble, and that was good. I wasn't in the mood for it, and I think that showed.

I finished our business with the sheriff. I took in all his information, just like I was planning on seeing he got that expected reward.

We sold our horses to some townsfolk at a loss, and then we were given some gas, as everyone thought highly of us all of a sudden, and I put it in my car. I cleaned the chicken shit off my windshield, and we rode out of there while people on the sidewalk cheered us.

On the way to Choctaw's place, Rufus fell asleep.

Choctaw looked back at him.

"There ain't no one to say what Rufus did or didn't do, Nat. I think he learned his lesson. I mean, hell, hadn't been for him, you might have got shot up, if you told me right about what happened."

"I told you right. But he did break the law."

"I just got your word for that," he said, and grinned at me.

After dropping Choctaw off into the loving arms of Little Wind, who told me to go to hell, I drove me and Rufus to Fort Worth. I decided not to turn in Rufus, and said he had volunteered to help us. He ended up going to work for the Pullman cars a short time after that. He liked the work better than I did. He'd had enough of adventure.

Railroad was damn happy with me. I was given a job as a railroad detective for the next five years, and finally I went back and did a bit of Pullman work, then retired.

I still got that Browning and the auto-pistol to remember that bit of excitement up in the Oklahoma hills. Hootie Hoot has written up that shootout in their town history. Wouldn't you know it, it doesn't mention that the ones who killed the desperadoes were colored. We just became railroad law. They let the readers fill in the blanks, and the blanks most likely made us white.

The sheriff didn't get his reward, of course. He got arrested on account of my word, telling them he had been taking bribes from the Radiant Apple gang. It didn't stick, of course. But he didn't stay sheriff. He was removed from office and forbidden to hold any kind of lawman job. I think he is a janitor of some sorts in Lawton now.

When I got back to Big Sandy, I went over to where Lillian lived, knocked on the door. She didn't answer, but the door was unlocked. I slipped inside. Except for the big squeaky bed, the room was empty. Even the window shades were gone.

I thought about tracking her down, but the more I thought of it, the more I decided to let it go. I was only thinking of it because it's what I thought I should do, not what I really wanted to do. Still, I consider on her now and again. I hope she's happily married somewhere with a flock of kids and a nice fat husband with a nice fat bank account.

Rufus has done well. Choctaw and I haven't exchanged a word since I came back from Oklahoma. I like to think him and Little Wind are still living the good life on all that oil money.

A lot of the time, I just sit on the front porch of my house, not far from the rail lines, watching all those trains go roaring along, pulling my past after them, like a dead man being dragged behind a horse.

One last thing. I bought me some ducks and chickens and built them some nice pens and chicken-wire fencing around the property that gives them the run of my back two acres. I talk to them the way Ruthie did, and lately, now that I've learned better how to listen, I think maybe I hear them talking back.